THE LIBRARY OF
NETHERLANDIC LITERATURE

Egbert Krispyn, *General Editor*

Offered by Twayne as part of its world literature coverage, *The Library of Netherlandic Literature* complements the critical studies of Netherlandic writers which appear in *Twayne's World Authors Series.* Both the critical evaluations and the translations are edited by Professor Egbert Krispyn of the University of Georgia.

The Library of Netherlandic Literature, devoted to the literature of Holland and Belgium, includes translations of some of the finest fiction, drama, memoirs, and essays produced by Dutch and Flemish writers. The program consists of first translations as well as reprints of out-of-print volumes and will include both classical and modern works.

The project is directed to meet the demands of teachers and students of Netherlandic literature in American and British colleges and universities, while serving the literary appetite of the general reader as well. Cooperating with Twayne, the Foundation for the Promotion of the Translation of Dutch Literary Works will nominate titles for translation and publication by Twayne.

Previous works published in the series include an anthology, *Modern Stories from Holland and Flanders,* representing the new voices in Netherlandic literature, Louis Paul Boon's 1953 novel *Chapel Road,* and Anna Blaman's novel *A Matter of Life and Death.*

Egbert Krispyn, currently Professor of German Literature at the University of Georgia, has both editorial experience and an extensive knowledge of Netherlandic studies.

The critical studies of Netherlandic writers contained in *Twayne's World Authors Series* include volumes on Erasmus, Jean LeClerc, Multatuli, Spinoza, Hendrik van Veldeke, and on the contemporary scene.

THE LIBRARY OF NETHERLANDIC LITERATURE

Volume 4

The Coming of Joachim Stiller
By Hubert Lampo

Edited by

EGBERT KRISPYN

Hubert Lampo

The Coming of
JOACHIM STILLER

Translated from the Netherlandic
By Marga Emlyn-Jones

TWAYNE PUBLISHERS, INC., NEW YORK

THE LIBRARY OF NETHERLANDIC LITERATURE
published with the cooperation of the
Foundation for the Promotion of the Translation
of Dutch Literary Works

Egbert Krispyn, *Editor*

Volume 4

The Coming of Joachim Stiller, by Hubert Lampo

Copyright © 1974 by Twayne Publishers, Inc.
Library of Congress Catalog Card Number: 73-3954

ISBN 0-8057-3416-3

MANUFACTURED IN THE UNITED STATES OF AMERICA

They said to one another, "Did not our hearts burn within us while he talked to us on the road, while he opened to us the scriptures?"

Luke 24:32

Contents

Introduction

The expressionist movement in Germany which dominated the literary scene during the decade from 1910 to 1920 was on the artistic and cultural level the pendant of the First World War. It was a frenzied revolt against the stultifying atmosphere in all areas of life in the newly founded Reich, especially under Emperor Wilhelm II. But although expressionism was the product of specifically German conditions, its excitement and ferment appealed strongly to the younger generations of writers in Holland and Flanders. Partly due to the effect of the war and its chaotic aftermath, however, literary expressionism made its appearance in the Low Countries with a considerable "cultural lag"; in a modified form it played a role of importance there during the 1920's, after it had virtually ceased to exist in Germany. The foremost representative of the movement in the northern Netherlands, the poet and critic Marsman, in 1921 traveled through Germany but only succeeded in making personal contact with a few surviving, creatively not particularly prominent figures. By the end of the 1920's the literary tide in the Netherlands turned, and there followed a phase, lasting at least until the German occupation during the Second World War, which was characterized by a strong interest in realism and psychology. These were elements which the expressionists had vehemently rejected because they were incompatible with their preoccupation with the archetypal and metaphysical aspects of life and humanity.

Hubert Léon Lampo, who was born in the ancient Flemish city of Antwerp in 1920, reached his years of literary discretion when the expressionist decade had long faded into the past and the more down-to-earth style was firmly established. The prevailing atmosphere naturally exerted significant influence on him and the direction in which his own budding talent developed. Nevertheless he was also to a remarkably high degree susceptible to the peculiar attractions of expressionism, to which he has devoted some of the best of his many essays. This affinity even goes beyond the realm of writing and amounts—as he once remarked himself—to "a strong

emotional relic of the atmosphere of the twenties." He has, consequently, one foot in each camp and this dualism of his background
tends to set him apart from the majority of his contemporaries and
gives his work a very distinctive flavor of its own. The essential
bipolarity of his creative universe as evoked in *The Coming of
Joachim Stiller* and his other major epic works is consistent with,
and rooted in, his stance astride the expressionistic-vitalistic and
the realistic-psychological currents. From his early writings on, for
instance, his novel *Hélène Defraye* published in 1944, there is the
ever recurring juxtaposition of two realms: that of his everyday
characters' carefully observed and recorded actions and motivations,
and that of the Absolute, frequently in the guise of sublimated Eros.

As his literary career develops with great consistency of creative
purpose, these elements gradually assume a more philosophical
significance, reflecting a world view and an intellectual position
that are unmistakably Lampo's own, though firmly rooted in an
ancient heritage of Western thought. His affinity for mystically
oriented ideas was further stimulated by encounters with a number
of like-minded writers.

Especially important among these kindred spirits was his Flemish
compatriot Raymond de Kremer (1887–1964), a versatile and
prolific author who wrote popular juvenile adventure stories under
the name John Flanders, and French novels on magic and fantastic
subjects under the pseudonym Jean Ray. He was preoccupied with
the notion of "folds in space," which reflected his extensive knowledge of mathematics and provided a basis for his speculations on
the existence of a parallel universe; an anti-cosmos. Ray also was
interested in mythical and archetypal concepts along the lines of
Carl Gustav Jung's theories. Other aspects of his work are related
to the surrealism of André Breton, the grotesque romanticism of
E. T. A. Hoffmann and the supernatural fantasies of Gustav
Meyrink. At times his writing is reminiscent of Kafka. Through
this many-faceted oeuvre Lampo was introduced to some of the
most seminal currents in European literature, which soon began
to exert their influence on his own publications.

Another writer to whom Lampo owes much is the somewhat
older Flemish novelist Johan Daisne, who in his books also explores
the idea of a universe existing parallel to ours, and sees it as the
function of literature to establish a link between the two. Daisne

provided Lampo with the term "magic realism" that best describes their common creative attitude, and that he in his turn has taken over from the protean Italian author Massimo Bontempelli (1878–1960). In applying this designation to his own work, Lampo also reflects on its meaning and implications in his numerous essays and self-analytical studies. He stresses that magic realism is not just a literary manner that can be adopted or discarded at will, but "a purely existential mode of experiencing life and the essence of the cosmos." At the same time, however, he is careful to point out that his literary commitment to this attitude does not necessarily indicate a personal endorsement. This objective outlook enables him in his novels to present a balanced view, in which the magic and the realistic are juxtaposed on equal terms.

The Coming of Joachim Stiller is also in this respect a very good example of Lampo's distinctive art. The two levels on which the action proceeds, that of the everyday reality of a writer and journalist in the city of Antwerp, and the supernatural which increasingly intrudes into his existence, are skillfully interwoven. They merge in the love motif which, in the romantic tradition, assumes mystic overtones while rooted in the fundamental erotic experience. This central role of the relationship between the middle-aged protagonist and a young and pretty math teacher is especially clear in the mysterious chimes concert that suddenly fills the air during their first night together. The nature of the music as evoked in one of the most impressive scenes in the book, the fact that only the lovers can hear it, and the suspension of time while it takes place are unmistakable indications that the ancient concept of the music of the spheres has here been revived in a modern setting, symbolizing universal harmony as a state of perfection which fallen mankind can only approximate in love.

But man shrinks back from this revelation and tries to avert the intrusion of the mystic element into his existence. Almost willfully the characters reject the efforts of the enigmatic Joachim Stiller to establish contact with them, trying to explain him away with all kinds of theories and assumptions, psychological, astrological, and even political. Their reluctance to accept the redeeming figure of Stiller and their tendency to rationalize his apparent omniscience and omnipresence make the final recognition of his true nature all the more effective. At the end, the allusions to the biblical account of His previous death and resurrection get, perhaps, a little obtrusive, but this scarcely distracts from the effectiveness of the final scenes.

At the same time, this novel is more than a literary expression of a metaphysical world view, and the realistic element does not only occur as a foil for the mysterious Stiller. In the true epic spirit, the author also dwells on details of everyday life, and evokes graphic impressions of the old town of Antwerp with its cafés, harbor districts, and people, as well as a nicely satirical image of a group of young would-be literary geniuses in all their immature pomposity. It is on this level that the narrative figure comes closest to identifying with the author, whose low-key tone and ironically tinged sense of proportion make a remarkable work of literature out of what, in less professional hands, could easily have deteriorated into a mere tract.

EGBERT KRISPYN

The Coming of Joachim Stiller

CHAPTER 1

The Resurfacing of Klooster Street

Although I work for a progressive paper I sometimes wonder whether I am not conservative by nature. Please do not misunderstand me. I do not mean it in the political sense of the word. Basically I am just a perfectly ordinary fellow who likes his food and drink and who, for the rest, quietly believes that mankind, by its own efforts, is gradually gaining its independence, as far as the pyromaniacs of this century will allow it. Personally I am convinced that no one can criticize my tendency to conservatism as being the result of a deplorable lack of strength. I sincerely wish my fellowmen the best, and not just on New Year's Day, yet at the same time demand my right to defend my inner world against any assault. Up till now I have always been fairly successful, and so I can testify from my own experience that an unremitting spiritual alertness is required for this which has not failed me for years. Not even the war shook my faith, however difficult it was for me to keep despair at bay when I learned of the arrest of my best friends and when later the news of their usually violent deaths reached me.

I felt in sympathy with the millions of mortals who suffered worse than I, yet entrenched myself stubbornly against the inner Horsemen of the Apocalypse, even when I joined the resistance and did not refuse a single reckless assignment, not even if I considered it absolutely without purpose. Yet those near me seem to think that in general I am easily upset. Ostensibly they are right, but the blows which I receive like everyone else have so far not affected my deeper being—at least, up to the moment when Joachim Stiller entered my life. It is probably nothing extraordinary, for where would we be if man did not have the resilience necessary to keep a certain equanimity? But no...that last statement did not tally altogether with what I, once and for all, wish to commit to paper; I am compelled to this by certain experiences about which

1

I am still at a loss but which, for the first time in my rather quiet life, shook my faith in the logical and materially conditioned cohesion of things.

For the sake of clarity I must draw attention to the fact that about three years previously I had given up living exclusively on my earnings as a novelist and critic. It is true that as a bachelor I succeeded in making ends meet, but finally it became too much for me that the ever hypothetical meeting of those ends appeared to depend mainly on the totally unpredictable sales of my books. Up to then I had written literary articles from time to time for *De Scheldebode* and when Clemens Waalwijk, the director, with whom I had worn out my first pair of long pants on the school bench, offered me a fairly well-paid job as city editor, I accepted without much hesitation. That, too, did not alter my inner perspectives. I have never understood why an author should turn up his nose at journalism. Waalwijk has done everything possible to please me and made sure that the broken arms and legs, the stolen bicycles, run-over dogs, lechers caught in the act, kleptomaniac lady store visitors and errant Sunday drivers remained in the domain of my younger editorial colleagues. When, however, events of a certain significance, as we say in our professional jargon, have to be reported, when an artistic matter is involved or generally when a description that is, to say the least, picturesque appears to be desirable, I am usually sent to deal with it. At first sight this may not seem important at all but in a time when the teleprinters spew forth most of the news into the editorial offices as good as ready for the press, a person like me is undeniably privileged. Clemens Waalwijk is an old hand in the trade who knows what's what. "It's not at all an unnecessary luxury to recruit someone like you for the more important local news service," he said. "Our potential circulation is mainly limited to this city of half a million inhabitants. Our competitors hope to make a big hit by imitating the tricks of international journalism. It's sheer nonsense. Not a soul is interested in the revolution in some obscure South American republic, and can one blame people if by now they scarcely read the big print over the heads of Mr. Eisenhower and Mr. Khrushchev? To us it's much more important that the dome of the Central Station—just to give an example—is about to collapse or that the statue of Rubens has disappeared without a trace. It seems nineteenth century, my dear fellow, but I am perfectly levelheaded in such matters and, as far as I'm concerned, a news service like this which is too genial at first sight is the only way to compete with radio and television . . . "

It sounded like the voice of common sense itself and practice has proved in the course of a short time—Waalwijk himself had been appointed only fairly recently—that my old schoolfriend was right. Our colleagues are complaining bitterly and are obliged to raise hell like a devil in a holy-water font with bazaars, competitions, or receptions of second-rate film actresses, in a desperate effort not to be completely swallowed up by some large trust. Our circulation on the other hand displays perhaps not a sensational but certainly an encouraging rising curve . . . All this is at first sight not particularly relevant to my story but my digressions are meant to be looked upon as fragments from a dossier. Not all are very important, I know, but each one taken individually contributes something toward shedding as much light as possible on the overall picture of the problem.

I am telling all this about my post on *De Scheldebode* purposely to make it clear to the potential reader how it came about that, as an old friend of the boss, I was given in addition a column—I notice now that I have still forgotten the most important thing—which I called, with a popular turn of phrase, "The Meditations of a Loafer," and which, though I say it myself, became remarkably successful, to judge from some of the readers' letters. I have enough self-knowledge, I think, to allow me to point out that a few traits in my character are most suitable for the writing of my two small daily columns. In the first place, I have always had, like many scrupulous people, an acute sense of the ridiculous. I could never find it in my heart to misuse it with purely demagogic intentions, but when I watch the grotesque behavior of some of my contemporaries, my senses react immediately and it is often difficult for me to keep the most drastic invectives, however picturesque and of whatever literary quality they may be, inside the keyboard of my typewriter. I have to reckon constantly with a sense of justice that some have even called morbid. It is true that both my sense of the ridiculous and the almost physical craving for justice do not always make it easy for me as a journalist at a time when our democratic society offers such excellent opportunities to selfish louts, intent on a quick profit; on the other hand, however, these qualities lend me a constant alertness which, I believe, belongs after all to an attitude of mind indispensable to the journalist who is genuine at least, however old-fashioned he may be. Clemens Waalwijk leaves me to do what I like and I appreciate this very much. Meanwhile it goes without saying that I am not always on my high horse: I'm just not a maniac. I can find material for articles in the most ordinary things, even if I find it more amusing to hold the present bureaucratic rule and the mushroom nobility of the voting urn up to ridicule. Each morning or afternoon, depending on circumstances, I set out for the city which lies close to my heart—I myself am not free from that local patriotism which sometimes gives Antwerp the bold mentality of an autonomous republic—and quietly keep my eyes open. The gaining of inspiration becomes in the long run something like an automatic process and up to now I have never lacked material. Anything can be the subject for an article: a traffic sign in a bad position, the new cars of the naval college, a shabby beggar who sells matches on a street corner in spite of our social legislation, the philistine reconstruction of a venerable antique façade, the appearance of the first summer dresses in our streets or a seventeenth-century, weatherbeaten statue of Our Lady in the rain.

It will not surprise anyone that I sit sometimes near the old lock that gives access to the inland port or on a terrace under the linden trees in a small intimate square behind the Dutch Theater, while less fortunate mortals busy themselves in the editorial office with their scissors and paste. Colleagues from other papers call me the "paid guest" of *De Scheldebode* for this reason, but I was quick in adopting the habit of introducing myself as such, and so it quite soon ceased being funny. Anyway, they are mostly pleasant boys, sometimes copper green on the outside, but usually made of bronze inside and we get on very well together. Such details are in fact not very important. I would not have dwelt on them, were it not for the fact that they form part of a world which, though to all appearances nothing has changed, I try to rediscover in vain, like Laertes on his return to Elsinore, and which I know deep down belongs irrevocably to the past, to a "time-span" that is gone, almost in the same sense as the Neolithic Age or the era of Pericles. By this I do not mean that I am not content with my new world.

Since there is always something or other to pick up in the slum quarters of the old city or in the dock area, my daily wanderings end usually in a popular pub in Klooster Street, called "Het gouden Anker." It is very quiet there, the beer is tapped with expert care, and I have a permanent seat by the window that is always wide open in the summer while it remains gloriously cool inside. Sometimes I write a bit there or I read a book about which I intend to produce an article: Waalwijk insisted that, even as permanent editor, I should not give up my literary contribution.

That fatal morning—a quiet, sunny, and happy morning nevertheless—I sat again in my permanent place and tried to lose myself in a recently published German study of Kafka. I found it difficult to concentrate, not only because the learned, but very dull, Herr Professor analyzed to fragments a world which had always seemed strangely familiar to me since my childhood, but also because mv attention was continually diverted by the morning bustle in this populous district. It was still quite early in the day and from where I sat I could see in the curve of the street the crowd standing out in a beautiful relief that would have enraptured any photographer, while I, in my turn, did not remain wholly indifferent to the sometimes enchanting thin summer dresses, treacherously transparent against the light. I still remember precisely that I had just ascertained from my wristwatch that it was half past ten, when a handcart appeared in my field of vision, and with it four men in working clothes. It struck me that they all looked young and vigorous, too handsome really for a job as extras in a streamlined American film or as models for the academy. They stopped on the opposite side of the street and planted two small red flags in the middle of the roadway, about twenty yards apart, so that it was easy for me to guess that they were preparing to tear up the cobbles. pride of our national quarries. I buried myself in my book again. A quarter of an hour later, when I looked up absentmindedly, they had already made quite a lot of headway. They piled up the cobbles on both sides diagonally across the street like a barricade. A policeman had sauntered up and raised his hand in command every time a car approached and finally became angry when suddenlv a long queue of cars were blowing their horns as if possessed. A group of children and some old men were now also watching the workmen with keen attention as they finished the removal of the

road surface over the whole marked area and sat down to eat their
sandwiches. When they had done that I expected them to start
digging to apply their industry to the water mains, gas pipes, or
the telephone or electricity cables, unless their task consisted of
cleaning out the sewers. In the meantime I noticed how at both
ends of the work area arguments were still going on between the
policemen—a second officer had appeared and was giving his
colleague a helping hand—and bad-tempered drivers. For a time
there was a big row with an oil truck on one side and a moving
van on the other, while behind them smaller vehicles raised a
deafening concert of horns. I tried to concentrate on my book
again, although I was distracted by the innkeeper who, dish towel
in hand, had taken up a post near the open window.

"Good God," he muttered, "have you ever in your life..."

In spite of myself I looked outside again and realized immediately
what he meant: the workmen, imperturbable as angels, conscious
of the uselessness of every gesture in the face of eternity, had begun
assiduously placing the cobbles neatly back in their original place
with the accompanying clatter of metal on freestone—a pleasant
and peaceful sound that had always given me a cheerful feeling
when I was a child. "It looked as though they were going to do
some digging," I said. "One gets the impression that it has only
been a superficial repair. It's high time that they asphalted these
old streets properly..." "That was no repair," the innkeeper laughed
scornfully; "take a look yourself, Mr. Groenevelt. It never was
such a pigsty before, and we pay taxes till we are blue in the face,
we pay..."

I thought to myself that at the next local elections the party of
the alderman for public works certainly ought not to count on his
vote. I watched closely—as if it was a very important matter—how
the men finished their job, loaded their tools on the little cart,
waved a cheerful good-bye to the policemen, and left quietly, glad
that their work was done for the day. After the disappearance of
these four proletarian Apollos out of the Belvedere the street seemed
quiet and unreal, all the more since the traffic seemed to avoid it
after the recent holdup.

"You ought to put that in the paper, sir," the innkeeper of
"Het gouden Anker" said. "It's a disgrace how our good money is
being wasted."

"You might have something there...," I replied.

I could not blame him. Behind his forehead, sturdy like that of a seventeenth-century chief of militia, the encouraging thought lived on, as with many of my open-hearted fellow citizens, that the papers are the prosecutors and consequently also the potential repairers of ignorance or injustice. We ought to take that more into account in our office, I think. Clemens Waalwijk could not have persuaded me of that more effectively.

CHAPTER 2

The Magazine Atomium

It was that same evening, if I remember rightly, that Andreas dropped in. I have lived, since the death of my parents shortly after the war, above an old and well-known druggist's shop on the top floor of a rather dilapidated but inhabitable renaissance house in Koepoort Street; it is not far from the harbor and, besides me, a few neglected painters live here, not to mention a spinster whose station in life was rather unknown. She wears elaborate morning dresses, hangs out a whole rainbow of nylon panties every week to dry in front of the window, and receives many gentlemen visitors without causing anyone the slightest inconvenience. It is very quiet and I lead a somewhat lonely yet peaceful bachelor existence under the rafters where tolerable chaos prevails, which the French sometimes call an *effet de l'art*. I do not receive many visitors. Usually, to avoid wasting time—some people, for reasons obscure to me, regard a writer as a sort of public institution—I make my business appointments in a pub called the "Antigone" on the Grote Markt, where many councillors come to drink their evening beer after sessions in the Town Hall and so at the same time I get the opportunity of gaining inspiration for my daily articles.

Only real friends are allowed inside—a principle of mine which stands me in good stead—and among them Andreas belongs to the old loyal friends for whom I am always at home.

That evening the rain poured from a sky as gray as in November and he thoughtfully wiped the raindrops from his glasses while he settled down comfortably in my worn armchair and I lay down unceremoniously on the enormous divan which I regard as the showpiece of my secondhand (and for that very reason rather decorative) furniture. His unexpected visit, despite the miserable weather, did not surprise me. He had turned to literature when he was no longer young and as a result revealed the same enthusiasm, now that his first novel was about to be published in Holland, as

8

I had done when I was twenty-five, more than twelve years ago.
Perhaps it is because of his enthusiasm which appears so youthful
and contagious to me that I like him so much and that I am always
pleased when he drops in for an evening. He always has a reason
for visiting me, however trifling. Sometimes he is brooding over
an idea for a novel about which he would like to know my opinion
or he has read a new or a very old book and wants to share his
enthusiasm with me. A visit from Andreas is never too much for
me, even when I am up to my ears in work, and so I rose after
a while from my beloved divan to get out the flask of gin. Because
of the heat inside—for days it had been sweltering and the rain
had only come now, at dusk—and also to increase the cozy atmosphere, I opened the window wide. There was absolutely no wind
in spite of the bad weather, so that there was something tropical
about the rain that poured down on the city with a soothing
murmur; from where we were we could see a hazy panorama of wet
roof tiles, covered by the sediment of centuries, and dilapidated
chimneys precariously balanced on them, a surprising view preserved intact from Brueghel's time, as I imagine, and above it the
profile of the Tower of Our Lady. It would be high tide soon, I
remembered, and out of the falling dusk we would hear the pre-
historic call of the boats on the Schelde—the Lemurian cry, I
sometimes called it, with an image obscure even to myself—which
I enjoyed in advance, shivering slightly without asking myself why.
I gave Andreas a cigarette, filled my pipe, stretched myself out
again in my sultanesque posture and asked if there was anything
new to tell me.

"Nothing much," he replied.

"Well anyway, nothing much is more than nothing at all, so
let's hear why you have come to me through this terrible weather,
although friendship alone is enough for me too."

"It's really not worth the trouble," he said. "Do you know this
thing?" He produced a small stenciled pamphlet, folded in two,
from his waistcoat pocket.

"No idea," I muttered vaguely.

"A new magazine of the younger generation," he went on,
"Volume one, number one. The thing itself is not worth bothering
about but you are discussed again for a change, on the first page,
in the editorial declaration of principles. Read it for yourself..."

The whole thing left me stone cold. As a result of my critical contributions and, even if I say so myself, my relative success as a novelist, the young whippersnappers of the day regularly make me the punching bag on which to try out their strength when they wish to give vent to their little inferiority complexes. To put it in a way clear to those who have lived through the war: anyone can be a Jew to someone. It is healthy for them and it does not trouble me, I think. It is not that I am above it; I just live with it. Nevertheless, I settled down comfortably and quickly read through the rather insignificant document that smelled of ink and cheap paper; it reminded me of the magazines that I myself had edited and circulated among my friends when I was a schoolboy. I actually lost myself in affectionate memories but Andreas was fidgeting in his seat because I was not impressed by what I had only glanced over anyway. The memory of my high-school days evidently made me smile involuntarily.

"You even seem to think that it's funny," he said scornfully, somewhat irritated by my apparently blasé attitude. "Come on, give it to me and I'll read it to you. I found the thing this morning among my mail together with the request to become a subscriber immediately, if I wished to cherish my self-respect any longer. I've been blazing with anger all day. Thank you... Listen, here it is: 'Not only will there appear regularly in the magazine *Atomium*— symbolic title for the spirit of the present era—work by young men of letters who up till now have not been given a chance in the official magazines, calcified products of a gerontocracy that is as ridiculous and treacherous as it is helpless, but we shall also join battle inexorably with those who for far too long have been accustomed to prostitute our literature in the guise of a dubious authority.'"

"Not badly written," I said. "That man knows how to use his adjectives." "That's not all," growled Andreas; "the best part is still to come. 'We think in the first place of our so-called eminent fellow citizen, Freek Groenevelt'—that's you," he informed me rather superfluously, looking at me over the rim of his glasses, embarrassed about what followed—"'whose dilettantism we will shout from the rooftops from this moment on and whom we will expose directly as the most hopeless bungler of all and the most utter literary pig who ever handled a ball-point pen in this country, forever intent on throttling any youthful talent in order to remain himself the unquestioned one-eyed king in the land of the blind...' "

My friend became visibly agitated as he was reading the prose of the youngest generation. As far as I am concerned, my antecedents go back far enough for me to be completely unperturbed by being called among other things an "artistic whore," a "literary afterbirth," and also by being depicted as a "senile old man, slobbering with impotence at every new, especially modernistic, sound," and other such pretty expressions which are by no means new to me, for that matter. The article, in which the malice lost its sharp edge, I felt, through its naïveté—an inevitable property of youth—was concluded with the stalwart assurance that my empire would soon be at an end. After that a number of colleagues who were considered to be of better repute were held up to me as an example—without thereby giving me a chance of rehabilitation, it was added; they were men like Willem Elsschot, Boontje, Jan Walravens, Hugo Claus, and Gaston Burssens, really great and progressive artists without inhibition or fear who were apparently disgraced by the very fact of my existence.

"Well," I chuckled, "that's that. I really ought to jump through the window at once. But let's have another drink on it."

"What do you say about such a bunch of scoundrels?" growled the other, obviously irritated by my good humor and calm. "Well, what do you say?" Andreas, whose complexion betrayed a plethoric nature even in normal conditions, had turned purple with vexation.

I shrugged my shoulders and filled his glass.

"I've already told you that the article is not badly written. There are quite a few members of the Society of Authors who would do worse."

"You don't have to play the big strong man with me. I came through the rain because I could not bear the thought that tomorrow some swine or other would enjoy rubbing this filth into you. I think it is a dirty trick and you ought to do something about it, if you ask me."

"Nonsense," I said, amused, but also slightly irritated that Andreas demanded my attention so emphatically for such essentially private trifles. It always depresses me when others, however well-meaning they are, try to influence me and attempt to prescribe a certain course of action for me. "Not a week goes by that I'm not abused and reviled a couple of times. For one you're too old, for the other too young, too left or not left enough, and if it's not that, you bump into some lout who doesn't like the color of your tie or thinks your nose is too long. Some fellow wrote to me during the war to say that it was high time for me to be sent to a reeducation camp in view of my complete lack of responsibility and patriotic feeling. There is not much left on this subject that I could get upset about..."

"You must do something," urged Andreas, "you cannot ignore something like this. These brats want a kick in their asses, otherwise they regard you as trash. Why should you not use your right of reply?"

"Come on, my dear Andreas," I said, "one does not reply to such things; surely we are not adolescents?"

"Write an article in *De Scheldebode* then," the other kept on. "You could turn a thing like this into a very nice article—something about good manners in art, the irreconcilability of the succeeding generations or heaven knows what. You are the journalist—not I. But you've got to shut these little whippersnappers up. It wouldn't be difficult for you to wipe the floor in five minutes with such kids. I'm telling you this out of friendship. You know how sincerely I appreciate your work," (he ignored my embarrassed protest at his praise) "and I think it's scandalous that it's precisely *your* name that's dragged in the mud by any piss-ant that comes along... I say, Freek, why is it?" he added suddenly after a short pause in a surprised tone of voice, as though he had overlooked something very important up to now. "What have you done to offend all those toddlers?"

"I don't know... A woman once told me that I was haughty, completely antisocial and that I have the objectionable habit of looking straight through people, as if they do not exist for me. Perhaps it's that? Anyway, I'll be damned if I am going to use that filth for my paper. I write on principle only about things from which the reader can profit. Your sympathy touches me, believe me, but there's no material whatever in this story for the daily press..."

"I don't understand how you can remain so indifferent..."

"We must never think ourselves more important than we are, old boy. Please don't regard this as affectation. It really is not important at all what a completely unknown young man thinks of me or my work. Sometimes in my car, when I have just managed to evade some reckless pedestrian at my own peril, I abuse him at the top of my voice. The poor wretch doesn't know what I think of him at that moment and there is not a single reason to suppose why there should be any common inner standard between us. I feel something like that pedestrian, you see?"

I sat down on the window ledge and looked down on the rainy street where the uneven cobblestones glistened under the light of the street lamps and the shop windows, while I tapped my extinguished pipe against the window frame until it was empty. The floor trembled perceptibly when a truck drove past and filled the narrow passage below almost completely. Suddenly the disturbing feeling stole over me—an inexplicable impression, yet not altogether unfamiliar to me—that I had in fact been fooling Andreas, that my imperturbability had given way under the roar of the accelerating diesel engine and that the sediments of all sorts of vexations, injuries, disillusionments, insinuations, and backhanded attacks had spread suddenly through my whole being like the dregs in an inexpertly handled wine bottle. It was high time to switch on the light but I preferred the twilight for a while with only Andreas's cigarette lighting up at regular intervals. I have known defeats like this since childhood. At first you feel strong and unassailable; it seems nothing is able to harm you from now on, until something deep inside you seems to snap off and you are left with only your solitude and a poignant realization of your own human limitation.

"Well," Andreas said peevishly, "I'll be off then. I didn't want to disturb you. It's your business but I would have thought that..."

"Oh, come," I interrupted him in a conciliatory tone, "I really didn't mean to underestimate your good intentions. Please stay. It's early yet. You would be doing me a favor. I have still got a few bottles of Scotch in stock which I have saved especially for you."

I switched on the light and went into the kitchen to look for clean glasses, after which we took our places by the open window, feet on the wrought-iron rail that had been put there for safety above the low window ledge. For a while we sat in silence listening to the gurgling of the water in the drain pipes. Finally I asked him, not without aversion:

"Well, what are we going to do about those *Atomium* boys?"

"I'm silent as the grave," Andreas said. "Basically you are right. Let them stew in their own juice."

"All in all I have the feeling that we've been talking beside the point, you see..."

"How do you mean?"

"I have been worrying for some time about two things. The first is that you don't need to react only to an insult that touches you deep down. You could react out of principle, if only to prevent uncivilized behavior always having the last word."

"There you are..."

"Secondly, the energy of some young man who is perhaps not even devoid of all talent and who will probably become wiser in time, need not always lead to a controversy, the unpleasantness of which goes against my nature, even if I don't have an exaggeratedly high opinion of myself..."

"I only thought that you ought to do something. What precisely I don't know myself. I suggested what came into my mind at that moment. But you are right. Polemics would go too far. They would be proud of it too."

"Well, I wonder how a lad like that would react if one went to see him, without any warning or ceremony. Not to quarrel, but to ask him quietly, man to man, what got into him."

"He'd be terrified, I'm sure he'd be frightened to death."

"He doesn't need to die of fright to please me," I went on, "but I think it would be an interesting experiment. The man must not get the impression that one wishes to convince him of one's own excellence..."

"No, the most important thing, Freek, is to make him think that he has made you curious."

"Fundamentally you are right there too," I answered. "Such things sometimes do make me curious. Suddenly it becomes apparent that someone whom you don't know at all and whom you therefore have not crossed in any way, hates you with a vehemence that is totally out of proportion... So you put on your hat and walk up to that potential arch-enemy to ask him what's the matter. Does that sound reasonable or am I letting my feelings run away with me?"

"It is Reason itself. He'll eat out of your hand, if you ask me. Do you intend to do it?"

"The idea appeals to me. If I can have that paper for a moment

I'll write down the address of the editor straightaway," I said, not quite certain whether the Scotch, added to a considerable dose of gin, was affecting me.

In any case, when, around midnight, Andreas made his intention clear to be getting along, I phoned for a taxi—just to be on the safe side.

CHAPTER 3

Alderman in the Dumps

A few days later Clements Waalwijk phoned me and asked me to drop in at his office some time. He was sitting behind his kneehole desk, grinning broadly, with his unfashionable horn rimmed glasses pushed up on his forehead; he looked like a flyer from the heroic age who had just climbed out of his primitive biplane made with a lot of rope and canvas. "Listen," he said, fiddling with the telephone cord and noticeably bored, "please do not think that I want to scold you, but you must listen to me for a moment."

"I am all ears," I answered, "go ahead. Why are you putting me on the carpet?"

"It's not very important but I think you ought to know. It is about your little article on that resurfacing in Klooster Street. No... don't interrupt. I can appreciate these fits of ill-temper, you know. One must be able to flare up from time to time when people get up to some stupid prank. It gives the reader confidence in his little paper, even if it rarely does any good. To me it is a question of mental hygiene, if I may call it that."

"Excellent," I interrupted my old schoolfriend, "and what is it exactly that is wrong with my article?"

"Read it for yourself," he said, and handed me a letter on which I immediately recognized the municipal coat of arms in the top left-hand corner, with beside it a nude lady and an equally nude gentleman. I read that the alderman for public works had, to his great surprise, taken cognizance of a slanderous article that had appeared in *De Scheldebode* entitled "Whom Are They Kidding?" in which useless repairs, supposed to have been undertaken recently in Klooster Street, were criticized. The alderman continued by saying that he insisted on accuracy and consequently drew the attention of the director of *De Scheldebode*—a paper nevertheless generally appreciated for its reliability—to the fact that not a single repair of road surface in the above street had been undertaken; and that he

16

therefore requested the esteemed editor not only to print a corrective statement but also to take care in future that contributors would indulge no more in the spreading of similar inaccurate, if not downright slanderous, reports.

I chuckled over the masterpiece of officialdom, the more since I knew that the alderman, a real estate agent by trade, was a rather helpless little old man who became indignant perhaps only in prose like this.

"Yes, I agree," smiled Waalwijk, "it's better to laugh than to cry about something like this. But anyway, Freek, do me a favor and don't invent stories like that in future. You know very well that I do not check you on the number of lines you write. I am not a grocer, you know that."

"Of course I know that," I answered, irritated because there was nonetheless something censorious in his friendly tone of voice, "of course I know that. But that fellow is lying his head off. I saw with my own eyes what I described!"

"Could that letter then be . . . ?" Waalwijk wavered and raised his eyebrows incredulously.

"Let us not make a drama of it, Clemens," I said. "But just to please me phone the police station of that neighborhood and inquire which officers were on duty in Klooster Street on that particular morning. They will confirm to you in person that they had terrible trouble with the traffic for more than an hour for the very reason that the road was broken up over its entire width."

He dismissed my arguments with a wave of his hand.

"Don't be stupid. If you tell me you have seen it, you have seen it. No one can accuse me of not always being prepared to back up my colleagues."

"My word, you are," I answered and smiled at the sudden note of aggrievement in his voice. "And in my case it is not even a retreat you have to cover. That public-works fellow is mad, or maybe his staff are trying to make a fool of him."

"In any case, we are not going to give in that easily. We are not going to let those stupid peasants walk all over us with their dirty feet."

"I would not get upset over it," I suggested soothingly. "It is a pity, but one must always reckon with touchy people. The good man probably found our paper on his desk in the morning, marked by some eager secretary, who hates the sight of his boss or is hankering after promotion. By the time he had the clerk responsible on the phone—let me go on imagining for a moment—he was probably so fed up that he only listened with half an ear. Moreover, you know how administration works. It is quite possible that the order for the so-called resurfacing still had to be put in writing officially, even when the job had already been completed. Or did those men perhaps pull up the wrong street and sneak off for that reason?"

Waalwijk had taken his glasses from his forehead and, using his handkerchief, was polishing them, apparently with close attention. Without this heavy thing with its black horn rims somewhere on the landscape of his face, even if only on his forehead, he looked naked and defenseless, in appearance at least, for I have rarely met anyone more sharp-witted than he. I waited until his eyes were again safely hidden behind the protective and strengthening shelter of a good number of diopters before asking what further action we ought to take and whether it would not be more sensible simply to throw the aldermanic missive into the wastepaper basket.

"No, damn it," he said, "I am not going to let this pass. It is a symptom, you see, the expression of a post-fascist mentality which became the order of the day after the war. The press is far too tame, forever frightened to scald itself with cold water while our so-called leaders seem to think that they can order us around too."

"Agreed, and . . ."

"We shall give that letter a suitable follow-up," he said in a more businesslike tone of voice. "We shall simply print it with the rest of your column, and add a postscript inviting our most esteemed alderman for public works to prove to us that on . . . what date was it again?"

"The thirteenth, I think . . ."

"To prove to us, as I said, that on the thirteenth of July Klooster Street was not pulled up. If the road surface looks enough of a mess you could send one of the photographers along. If you can provoke letters from readers, or interview the officers involved, so much the better. What do you think?"

"A lot of fuss over nothing," I replied, "or at least over almost nothing, but I am actually beginning to enjoy this. Shall I go and see the man?" He looked at me dreamily and rubbed his forefinger straight along his nostril. Then he picked up the phone resolutely and ordered the operator to put him through to the Town Hall. I admired the mixture of succinctness and ironic humor with which he kept the alderman in suspense after having dismissed some lower official rather brusquely. When I got up to leave him alone during the conversation, he gestured that I should remain seated; and later he seemed to be making a game of leaving the other uncertain about the question whether I would go to him to offer him my humble apologies or, on the contrary, as an authorized messenger not only of an editorial staff whose professional honor had been deeply offended, but also of thousands and thousands of avid readers, thwarted in their praiseworthy craving for truth by his, the alderman's, official protest.

When I entered the office of Alderman Keldermans, impressive in its late renaissance style, I seemed to leave my aggressiveness behind at the doorstep, as if I had handed it over to the usher together with my raincoat. The whole business seemed suddenly completely inane. All at once I could not understand what had come over Clemens Waalwijk and myself too, for that matter.

He was a little gray man whose age was difficult to determine; he wore an old-fashioned pince-nez and his jacket badly needed pressing, which I found rather endearing. He looked at me as if he expected me to give him an undeserved thrashing; this disarmed me almost completely and made me feel well-disposed toward him.

"Mr. Alderman," I said in a tone that was aloof, yet prepared for reconciliation, "I am terribly sorry to disturb you. It is true that your letter has taken my chief and especially myself by surprise but now I wonder nonetheless if it is worth the trouble to worry you about something like this."

He waved assiduously with his pale hands which in the dim room reminded me of erring night moths surprised by the first light of dawn.

"On the contrary," he said in a frayed voice, and I felt like telling him to clear his throat, "on the contrary, Mr.... eh ... What was it again?"

"Groenevelt, Freek Groenevelt, just like the author..."

"On the contrary, Mr. Groenevelt. Sit down. Do you smoke?"

I took a cigarette from the case he held out to me. Before I could find my matches he stood ready with a light.

"You see, Mr. Groenevelt, I am of the opinion that the authorities must cooperate as closely as possible with the local press."

I nodded understandingly, as if he had proclaimed a great truth full of profound meaning.

"It is exactly for that reason that I asked my chief to request an interview with you."

"Well, well," he doddered, as if I had parried his Einsteinian reflections with a formula of Heisenberg to whom he himself had not yet aspired. I suddenly had an irresistible craving for a morning beer and in my imagination I was already in the old-fashioned tavern "De Vos" on the opposite side of the Grote Markt where they know the secret of tapping noble local brews, highly fermented and intended mainly for local consumption, at exactly the right temperature and with precisely the right amount of froth on top.

"You see, Mr. Alderman, fundamentally I am convinced that your letter is based upon an error. But rather than going on about it in the paper"—it sounded like a veiled threat, but it would be foolish to be too kind, I thought—"I came to tell you personally. It was an impulsive reaction of mine which in retrospect I find rather presumptuous."

"Not at all, not at all, Mr. Groenevelt. It is good that you have come. But why are you, like Mr. Waalwijk just now on the telephone, talking so persistently about an error?" He put his nightmoth hand, as if taking an oath, on a document that lay before him on the enormous renaissance table. "There is no question of an error, Mr. Groenevelt, surely you ought to know that? I have here the report of my technical staff. You can see that I am not just talking. It says quite clearly in the report, in black and white, that your article, eh...forgive me"—he seemed suddenly very embarrassed—"that your article has no foundation in fact at all."

In spite of myself I bent over toward him leniently, as one does toward a child that tells lies obdurately and that one wishes to correct in a gentle manner. Not altogether without sympathy for the nervous, gray little man on the other side of the writing table, I said slowly:

"It has been printed, likewise in black and white, in about two hundred thousand copies of De Scheldebode how, on the thirteenth of July, without apparent reason and definitely without any use-

ful consequence, part of Klooster Street was broken up. Quite a
few children, passersby, and loiterers were watching, while at least
two police officers witnessed the scene. I am the man who wrote
about it and I do not withdraw a word, not even a comma, of it.
However, I do not doubt your good faith, Mr. Alderman. But I
know that many an outsider cannot be talked out of the idea that
journalists are queer customers, perhaps not quite right in the head.
I have never suffered any abnormality, as far as I can remember, that would make me doubt the things I see happening before
my eyes. Anyway, hallucinations do not leave traces behind of cobblestones that have been put back in a hurry."

During this argument that was far too emphatic and quite contrary to what I had intended, I thought to myself: "This is an idiotic
situation. Why attach so much importance to an event that is of
no consequence at all? What kind of inexplicable obstinacy has
got into us?" The other sat staring in front of him, hunched up,
disheveled and appearing suddenly overcome by panic. I felt really
sorry for him and thought myself an uncouth bear, even almost a
swindler who tries to blackmail helpless elderly gentlemen. He
could not have looked more miserable had I come to him with the
knowledge that in an unguarded moment he had molested a typist
under age. He looked plainly wretched and hardly seemed to be
taking my presence into consideration, as if fascinated by things he
alone could see. Unspeakably bored by the whole situation, I
said, "Are you not feeling well, Mr. Alderman? Can I do anything
for you?" He looked at me as if most surprised by my presence,
though he appeared to be making a strong effort to remember my
face. Meanwhile I had got up. I did not feel at all comfortable in
this first act of a bad comedy. If the usher had come in unexpectedly,
he would undoubtedly have thought that I had maltreated the old
man. I tried to draw his attention to the fact that I was taking my
leave, but he beckoned me with his pince-nez that had fallen off
his pointed nose and was dangling at the end of a ribbon, and thus
expressed his desire that I should sit down again. He looked at me
with so much helpless urgency that I could not bring myself to
leave him to his fate. He walked, feet dragging, to a baroque writing
desk of romantic workmanship full of foliage and putti, produced
a bottle of Courvoisier and two large glasses, and gave me a sidelong glance full of complicity, as if I had caught him out in a

secret sin. He filled the globular glasses in silence and it was in silence that we emptied them in one draft. It appeared to do him a world of good.

"I am sorry, Groenevelt," he said, clacking his tongue involuntarily like a connoisseur, "but I did not in fact feel too good."

"You are getting excited over a matter of no consequence, Mr. Keldermans. I am sorry in my turn that I have given rise to this. You seem to regard the case as a matter of life or death. Surely that is nonsense?"

I had the feeling for good and all that I was walking over a freshly tarred road in which my soles kept getting stuck, or through a labyrinth in the fun fair; I wanted to get out but irrevocably got further and further lost in it.

"Please do not blame me for that letter, Groenevelt," he mumbled, after filling the glasses once again. "The letter was a measure that unfortunately I could not do without, but please keep it to yourself. It is a secret between you and me and it ought to stay that way..."

"I am completely baffled," I replied, hovering between the jolly tone of a tippler and the mezzo voce of a light-shunning conspirator.

"No," said the other, whose cheeks were flushed like those of a nineteenth-century ingénue with spots on her lungs, "no, I can understand that you are at a loss." He bent over to me, leaning his elbows on his desk, and whispered hoarsely: "It is a conspiracy. It is not the first time something like this has happened. Do you understand?"

"You don't say?" I was really grinning now. "I still do not understand. I am obviously being rather stupid today. Are you perhaps making a habit of sending crazy letters like that to the editors of daily newspapers?"

"That is not what I mean, Groenevelt. Not the letter. I mean the other thing. Klooster Street. Of course I have not doubted the truth of it for a moment!"

"Why then make me out to be a liar to my director? Is that perhaps what one usually calls politics?..."

"You must try and understand me, Groenevelt." I thought I could hear him panting softly like some dogs do, hours before a thunderstorm breaks out. "It is perhaps incomprehensible to you, Freek, but you must try." Was his sudden familiarity a sign of sincerity? "I knew that it was true but nevertheless I had to protest against such a disconcerting and alarming truth..."

"Alarming? What put that idea into your head? You are drunk— we both are, for that matter."

"I can take more than a few of these miserable glasses, Groenevelt. But remember what I am going to say... There are things going on that frighten me. But no, forget it. I had to write that letter because I had no choice. Because I did not want Klooster Street to be broken up..."

"A case of nerves," I thought to myself. "One thing is certain, literally or figuratively speaking, he has had a blow on the head. The public works are in good hands if you ask me... I have to get out now, otherwise I shall go mad myself."

And aloud, distantly again, I concluded, "I respect your motives in every way, Mr. Alderman. Yet at the same time I take the liberty of supposing that we have agreed to let the matter rest, let sleeping dogs lie and not mention it again in *De Scheldebode*. I shall tell my director that your protest was based upon an administrative error."

This time I did not wait for his reply, but nodded good-bye, ignored the helpless gesture with which he tried to restrain me again, and left the office in such a hurry that it was more like a flight; the usher, who had been dozing, watched me with surprise and had to run after me with my raincoat.

CHAPTER 4

The Letter from Joachim Stiller

In the square of the open window the panorama of the city lay trembling in the sun, as in a color movie before the camera begins to travel. I put the milk bottle and the mail on the table and went to take a shower. Then I sat down to breakfast and, sipping my hot coffee, glanced through the correspondence; I had found it as usual under the milk bottle—a small favor which the lady who lived below did me, though she had not yet made it an excuse to try to get to know me better. There was a copy of the magazine *Atomium* on which I spent no further thought, a circular for a new edition of an encyclopedia, a picture postcard from Florence from my publisher, a contract for a radio lecture, some proof sheets, and a letter without the usual mention of the sender on the back of the envelope. I opened it with my table knife, crumpled the envelope up into a ball, and threw it into the wastepaper basket. While I took a bite from my French roll, I used my free hand to smooth the folds of the letter; it had no date, which surprised me a little, and in it I was addressed straightforwardly as "Dear Mr. Groenevelt." It was a rather short message which went as follows:

On July 14, 1957, you will publish an article in the daily newspaper De Scheldebode concerning repairs carried out on the road surface in Klooster Street. When you receive this letter this article will already have been published. Although you will find my interest in this matter extraordinary or at least out of all proportion, I do thank you for the attention given to this apparently unimportant event. It heralds other phenomena about which I prefer to remain silent for the moment. Perhaps some people will blame you for your article, but I believe that you are equal to this. If in the near future other events occur which in your opinion do not correspond with generally accepted logic, never doubt the precise detail of what you have seen or perhaps heard. As for me, you will not be out of my sight, whatever may happen to you. Yours faithfully.

24

After which followed, clearly legible, the signature *"Joachim Stiller."* I shrugged my shoulders and poured out another cup of coffee. Being a journalist, I knew that letters like this arrive almost daily in the editorial office from maniacs, world improvers, or neurasthenics. They are not answered and usually nothing more is heard from the senders, unless they belong to the smaller category of persistent people who indeed do not seem to expect a reply but nevertheless keep sending letters at irregular intervals. Written in the clumsy scrawl of the practically illiterate, full of mistakes in language and spelling, they are epistles one cannot make head or tail of. It could therefore not escape my notice that my completely unknown correspondent expressed himself stylistically quite well, that his handwriting was devoid of all pathological traits, and that he indulged in no way in the usual repetitive gibberish I knew so well from those rather depressing documents.

Although I forced myself to devote my attention exclusively to the fried eggs, I found myself staring over my plate at the piece of paper with its lengthwise and diagonal folds. Why deny that I was suddenly pretty fed up? I stirred my coffee irritably and reflected that even a cultured person could after all be crazy. At first sight this Stiller could be a retired teacher or something like that. His steady, experienced handwriting gave me this impression, together with the absence of the superfluous scrolls and flourishes so typical of illiterates who make a special effort. From the use of the old-fashioned, supple pen with its sharp point I thought I might conclude that my strange correspondent was of an advanced age; I myself had no longer used that kind of pen at school, thirty years ago. I could hardly deny that the incident irritated me. Of course I did not doubt for a moment that it was all the work of an eccentric or some tasteless joker. The content, however clearly written, was preposterous. But the vague feeling of unease had also something to do—I suddenly became aware of this—with the form of the paper, a perfectly ordinary ruled quarto sheet which one can buy in any stationery shop or general store. And it was also connected with the ink which was not quite black or dark blue, but slightly faded and brownish. I picked up the letter again and felt it carefully between thumb and forefinger in the same way as bank clerks, I believe, check the authenticity of notes. "Damn it all!" I swore suddenly aloud, "I must be mad!" and threw the letter angrily on the table after which I crossly buttered another roll. Usually I attach great importance to my breakfast and enjoy it quietly on my own, but that morning my pleasure was spoiled. I dislike anything that clashes with my customary routine, however well I am able to adapt myself to the unexpected element in the life of a journalist; for that matter, it is an inevitable consequence that after a period of time the unexpected in our profession becomes a habit in its turn. If, in the event of a colleague's sudden illness, I had a telephone call from the paper telling me to be ready within an hour for a publicity flight by some airline to Honolulu, I would have been less upset by it than by that damned Stiller and his stupid little scrawl. I finished eating without any appetite and then stood by the open window with my hands in my pockets, smiling scornfully. The sky rose up as in a watercolor above the rain-washed red rooftops, and only a few wisps of cloud trailed in the direction of the Schelde. Very high up in the blue sky an inaudible jet made a sharp white track that afterwards slowly faded away. From the street below the cheerful sounds of the morning rose up; washing had been hung out to dry in the most impossible places and wherever I glanced through a window I saw housewives quietly getting on with their work. I filled my first pipe of the day and watched the coils of smoke with satisfaction, enjoying the summer morning in spite of myself.

The moment I realized that I was no longer worried about the letter—and then it was too late, of course—it suddenly dawned on me that I had thrown the envelope into the wastepaper basket. It was not difficult for me to find it again, all crumpled up. I carefully smoothed it out on the window ledge and, completely perplexed, stared at the stamp. It was a specimen that I remembered vaguely from my earliest childhood; it had been out of circulation for at least thirty years and still had the popular war portrait on it of King Albert with his trench coat and helmet on. While reflecting that every serious collector probably had the complete series in his album and that they were moreover still for sale in every philatelist's shop, my gaze fell on the date stamp. I literally rubbed my eyes in amazement. The stamp itself, like the ink, was slightly faded, but there could be no doubt that it was completely intact. Dismayed I read: II.IX.19., from which could be deduced by means of logic—insofar as one could talk about logic in this affair—that

the letter must have been posted about a year and a half before
my birth...I can appreciate a joke, but I have an instinctive
aversion for what the Americans call the "practical joke"—explosive
cigars and suchlike, and I feel the same about anonymous (or as
good as anonymous) letters—for what did the name Joachim Stiller
mean to me after all?—not so much because of the harm they do,
but because of the vague kind of primeval fear they arouse in me.
In brief, I would have preferred a notice of assessment from the tax
collector to this idiotic message, written by some pathetic joker or by
a lunatic schoolteacher who had obviously read too many detective
stories. It is true, I did not doubt for a moment that it was an innocent letter, even a rather friendly one, but it filled me with an
amorphous uneasiness, for it troubled me that an unknown person
evidently wanted to force his way into my existence and that my
strongly defended frontiers, full of barbed wire, dragon's teeth,
and hedgehogs which I had put up around myself, were in this
case of no avail to me.

Once again I read through the enigmatic text. For a moment I
felt I had made an important discovery when I noticed that apparently all those words had been carefully avoided whose spelling
had been somewhat modified since the war. But how could I be
certain that it had been done on purpose?...I thought myself most
ridiculous, yet did not feel able to think about anything else for
the present. At last, in a bad temper, I decided to walk to the
newspaper offices—I left the car in the garage on purpose—where
the name Stiller, which in any case I could not find in either the
telephone or street directories of the city, might not be unknown.
Unless it was my colleagues themselves who wanted to pull my leg,
and if so, they would certainly get no pleasure from it, they could
count on that...

I hesitated on the landing of the second floor. Then, inspired
by a sudden brainstorm, I rang my neighbor's bell, although her
rather abandoned way of life had kept me at a distance up till now.
It was not long before the door was opened. I had just time to look
at the carefully polished copper nameplate to ascertain that the
occupier of the second floor was known by the exceedingly bour-
geois name of Maria Vandecasteele. My unexpected visit surprised
her, yet she did not seem disconcerted by it.

"Do come in, Mr. Groenevelt," she said hospitably, "please excuse everything being so untidy..."

"I am sorry, Madam, to disturb you so early," I replied. "I shall not keep you long."

Her apartment was furnished in petit-bourgeois taste and gave not the slightest impression either of material or moral disorder. The wide-open windows also gave the impression that Maria Vandecasteele had nothing to hide from the suspicion of the outside world. She immediately closed the door of the adjoining bedroom, so that I only got a glimpse of an unmade bed with very clean sheets. She herself looked very neat in her dressing gown and carried with her the fresh fragrance of a woman who has just had her bath. Her hair had been tied for the present into a ponytail. I took her to be about thirty. We sat down and I accepted the cigarette she offered me, in spite of my dislike for the cork tip.

"Well," she said, after I had given her a light, "I'm glad that we are getting better acquainted with each other at last. How can I help you?"

I actually began to feel in a pleasant mood, mainly because, in spite of the conventional words, there was really nothing conventional at all in the situation—at least not in the way we have come to expect from books about would-be erotic adventures and second-rate films. Her dressing gown did not fall open accidentally while she bent forward under some pretext or crossed her legs, nor did she look at me defiantly from under downcast eyelashes or appear to be looking for an excuse to make it clear to me that she had nothing on under her morning dress—which was in point of fact quite possible, I thought to myself.

"In the first place, I would like to thank you for bringing up my correspondence so often. I am ashamed that I have not thanked you before."

"But that goes without saying...The box has no lock and the caretaker is not exactly discretion itself!"

"Further I would like to ask you if this letter was in fact among this morning's mail..."

I showed her the crumpled envelope.

"Of course, Mr. Groenevelt. I remember it because it has such a strange stamp. To be quite frank, I thought of asking you if I could have it for my little son."

"I would prefer to keep this envelope intact for the time being," I said, as though I found the existence of a little son, probably boarded out or put up somewhere with relatives, quite self-evident. "But I can get as many stamps for you as you like. They only throw them away at the paper."

"You would do the child and me a great favor," she smiled gratefully, and I immediately got the feeling of being a very decent man.

My mood had improved considerably when I walked through the sunny city toward the editorial office. My vexation had now given way to an almost benevolent interest. I noticed no suspicious smirks or looks of mutual understanding among my colleagues when I asked the typist, quite naturally and within everyone's hearing, if letters from more or less crazy correspondents were preserved. Without the slightest trace of secret amusement or complicity in any plot, she produced three folders, a true anthology of epistolary schizophrenia. I was pretty well occupied with it for the greater part of the morning and I looked through all the letters one by one. A psychiatrist would have reveled in them. I did not come across either the handwriting or the name of Joachim Stiller who, in the course of a couple of hours, had taken on as it were mythical, although no longer vexatious, proportions. It was quite clear that none of my colleagues was interested in the question of who or what the object of my curiosity might be. True, they enjoy jokes, but their humoristic ideas are always accompanied by such obvious hilarity that there is never any question of sneakiness. I knew for certain now that I could write off the idea that they had wanted to make fun of me, even if they had heard something about the interview with Keldermans. But be that as it may, it was a joke in any case—no one could have the slightest doubt about that...

CHAPTER 5

Encounter with Simone Marijnissen

That evening, when I had finished work at the paper, I walked up
to the Schelde to eat in the old-fashioned restaurant on the promenade where one can enjoy a steak while overlooking the river.
When the waiter brought the coffee, the sky was already bathed in
the "Californian gold" about which one of our poets writes. But the
oily water on which a lonely tug, duty done, drew almost wearily
a slowly dissolving V-shaped track, had been of a dull purple color
since the disappearance of the sun which, in its last minutes far
away over the Flemish plain, had been red as in prehistory, I imagine, on the eve of the cosmic catastrophes of the Old Testament.
As I was paying my bill, a scrap of paper fell out of my wallet.
It was the address of the magazine *Atomium*. Resentfully I filled
my pipe. I am by nature fond of peace and solitude. Now that I
reminded myself of the conversation, steeped in old gin and a lot
of Scotch, I realized I had agreed with Andreas in the end because
I cannot endure strangers forcing their way uninvited into my
life. The boys of *Atomium* could proceed to raze my work to the
ground and I would not be in the least perturbed. It is part of the
unwritten laws and the—perhaps perverse—ethics of our profession.
I am not lacking in self-knowledge and critical sense. If I had to
review one of my own books I would certainly not give it a better
critique even than that of an unfavorably disposed colleague. But
for the rest I want to be left in peace; I do not tolerate attacks in
which strangers pass sentence upon me as a man, and I am prepared
to fight for that peace. I folded the piece of paper with the address
on it into a little strip and pushed it under the metal bracelet of my
watch. Leisurely I strolled to the garage where, between the trucks
of a transport company, my little car—a Citroën of the latest model
of which I am as proud as a peacock—occupies a modest place. It
was a quiet, almost provincial evening with little traffic, but with
many people on the front-door steps in the poorer quarters, like the
evenings of my childhood, mysterious and melancholy with the

singing of little girls, the subdued voices of the adults in the shadow
of the doorway or sometimes in the distance the blare of a march-
ing brass band. I followed trolley line 4 to its terminus on the
still rural church square of Hoboken. I had decided beforehand not
to search long for Linden Street and if necessary to be content with
a glass of beer on one of the crowded café terraces. I was not given
the time to ask myself if I really was intent on challenging those
Atomium sharpshooters in their den. The avenue I had turned into
at random was in fact Linden Street; and contrary to our national
custom of making any miserable old tree the pretext to promote every
row of houses in the neighborhood to "avenue" or "lane," Linden
Street really *was* an avenue which had apparently belonged to a
park in the past, when it was still the domain of some noble Antwerp
merchant family. There were many small villas which gave a
friendly impression with their shrubs and many lawns and flower
beds in the little gardens around them.

It was a country cottage in English style where I gently rang the
bell. A little while passed before I heard the quick sound of steps
as if someone was coming down the stairs. The door was opened
by a young woman.

"I am sorry, Madam...," I began like someone who has realized
too late that he is at the wrong address. "Does Mr. Marijnissen per-
hape live here?"—for that was the name of that editorial secretary
fellow, I remembered at the last moment.

"Mr. Marijnissen? That would be a bit difficult," the young
woman in the doorway said with a smile. "My name is in fact
Marijnissen, Simone Marijnissen, but I only rent an apartment here.
The people downstairs are called Jansen."

I am not so stupid that I did not see the light immediately. So
as not to make too miserable an impression I said, "Well, it is a
mistake then. Please forgive me. Of course it is not here that the
magazine *Atomium*..."

"It is, sir... How can I help you?" she interrupted me, apparently secretly amused by my clumsiness.

I had said A and now I had to go on with the alphabet.

"A friend gave me a copy of your magazine, you see. Please be
reassured, I am not a poet who cannot get his work published..."

On the landing hung a lower-middle-class smell of beeswax and
in the background the indefinable aroma that seems to give sub-

stance to the soul of some houses. But I knew that it did not belong to her apartment, even before she had opened the door on the second floor where the fragrance of the nearby park predominated—especially the perfume of the linden trees—and that of hay, put out to dry somewhere in this still rural district, which gave a sharp edge to the hazy evening air.

"I have been lying down and listening to some music in the dusk," she said. "I'll just switch on the light."

I could in fact hear the slow ticking of the needle in the last groove of a long-playing record. I imagined that on a fragile evening like this it must have been Mozart, but my inborn skepticism, aided by the habit I had acquired from experience never to expect things to be as harmonious as we prefer to imagine them, forced me immediately not to hope for more than Sidney Bechet or Charles Aznavour. When she had lit two low lamps which filled the room with an intimate clarity, and put the record away in the glossy yellow cover of the Deutsche Grammophongesellschaft, I noticed to my satisfaction that it had to be Bach. It made me feel restful, as if the music had left behind in the room an auditory shadow of its elysian mathematics; at the same time I realized that I had been overcome by a rather unbecoming nervousness while I climbed the stairs behind her and I had seen her splendid bare legs far above the folds at the back of her knees and the expensive lace of her petticoat. I could see now that she was a few years older than I had imagined in the dim light on the doorstep and in the corridor. But this weakened in no way the impression she made upon me—on the contrary. In her cotton summer dress the contours of her body were clearly visible, not so much what is called fully mature, but completely perfect, like a flower on the first morning of its bloom. My mood became lyrical. She had gray eyes which, I felt certain, would incline to purple or blue in daylight, naturally wavy brown hair twisted into a great coil—when she undid it, it would easily reach down to her hips, I reflected—aristocratic features which seemed to smile by nature, even when she looked serious, and there was an intriguing contrast between her discreetly yet expertly made-up lips and her brown summer skin. I wondered if she was short-sighted and had taken off her glasses out of female vanity. Afterwards I noticed that I had been wrong; which was due to the concentrated attention with which she looked at me—a look without suspicion, yet filled with an interest devoid of all obtrusiveness, that only few can find for their fellowmen. People sometimes praise an actor by saying that he can listen while others on the stage are talking. The same could also be said of her, and it was connected mainly with the way she looked about her.

She invited me to take a seat and sat down right opposite me under the light of one of the lamps. I now took her to be about twenty-five and felt completely at ease in her presence, although I did not have the faintest idea of how I would get to the heart of the matter—the totally unimportant matter. We looked at each other and laughed at the same time because of our silence that was, however, not at all forced. "Well...," I hesitated, "I really expected to meet a male editorial secretary and I did not have the faintest notion..."

"That it would be a female secretary," she completed the sentence for me. "Why should it make any difference? I am a teacher of mathematics at the Atheneum, accommodated for the time being in the old castle in the park. Most of the other people on the magazine are colleagues of mine." At my age, I felt vaguely uneasy that the younger literary whippersnappers were already teachers at the Atheneum with a right to a pension and family allowance. But I confined myself to muttering something vaguely in agreement. Fascinated, I listened to her pleasant, strikingly soft and rather dark voice and wondered if I should not simply save appearances and place an order for the magazine under Andreas's name, for example, and at his expense for a joke—that would teach him—only to disappear again just as anonymously as I had come. I suggested evasively, "It must be really amusing. I can imagine it very well, you know. All very smart young intellectuals who get on well together, fresh from the university and then their own magazine... It reminds me of my own younger days."

She looked at me with interest. It seemed to me that this time I detected something inquiring in her glance, not the latent hostility of someone who is on her guard, I mean, but a kind of removal in space, like an optic reaction to a psychic adjustment. I know now that it had been the delicious serenity of her voice which had filled me from the first words with an inexplicable melancholy.

"I appreciate your interest very much, sir. I hope you will not think me narrow-minded if I ask you..."

"What is the purpose of my visit?"

The hot smoke of my cigarette brushed past my fingernail. I would have felt more at ease if I could have lit a pipe right away. There was no escaping it any longer; all the cards had to be put on the table. "You understand perhaps...," she said with an apologetic gesture that gave me the impression of a beautiful choreographic movement.

"Of course I understand. After all, I am a strange fellow who drops in unannounced on a lady and does not even explain what it is all about. Are you angry with me?"

"Of course not," she interrupted me with the insistence of women who know very well that they are being misunderstood on purpose and yet uphold the appearance that it disarms them completely. "But who in my place, what woman I mean, would not be curious?"

"I expect it will be easiest simply to introduce myself, Miss Marijnissen. It is very late but I hope you will excuse me. My name is Freek Groenevelt."

She stubbed out her cigarette and answered quietly, this time however without looking up: "I knew it. I remember your photograph from the textbook of Dutch literature that I myself used when I was still a young girl at school." True, I felt slightly foolish, but my vanity was gratified all the same—I am moderately vain, but that is a secret between Vanity and me—for that photograph was most flattering, partly because in it I looked perhaps a little too young and theatrically passionate, a quality I have lost in the course of the years, although I do not yet belong to the category of middle-aged gentlemen with graying or thinning hair. If I were an actor—and often have I dreamt of being one!—my waist would, alas, no longer fit the role of Romeo, but I would still make a rather good Orsino. "If music be the food of love, play on, give me excess of it...," I quoted playfully to myself, and I would have appreciated it if she had switched on the gramophone again. She concentrated her gaze on her delicate hands.

"I ought to have thought of it," I came to her rescue. "I have no excuse. If I had not met a lady I would have said immediately what it was about. I would of course have introduced myself at once. But as it was I became confused. Please forgive me..."

"Would you have introduced yourself as Freek Groenevelt or as ... Joachim Stiller?"

Sometimes I give the impression, outwardly at least, of possessing an astonishing amount of self-control. It is only appearance that helps me, but I knew nevertheless that I looked at her merely with a tired glance.

"Where in heaven's name did you get such a mad idea?"

For the first time her voice sounded refractory, but I thought I could feel she was under some stress.

"I was under the impression that you had used this pseudonym more than once, Mr. Groenevelt."

"The name is not new to me," I replied slowly. "But I do not think that it matters. Had you been a Simon instead of a Simone, I would have asked you purely out of curiosity what the frantic hatred of your friends is based upon. But now I no longer think it to be of the slightest importance. Although you do not seem to trust me, I wish to emphasize that the name you mentioned"—something stopped me from repeating it—"belongs to someone who is completely unknown to me and who seems to take a curious interest in my affairs. I must say moreover that I find it impossible to express my surprise to hear you connect that name with me, yes, it is something so crazy that you cannot have any idea. I'm sorry ... I'm afraid I am not expressing myself very clearly ..."

It annoyed me to notice that I was becoming agitated. A drink would have done me good.

"Not very clearly, if you want to know my honest opinion ... ," she said in a conciliatory tone of voice.

"Yet it is not my intention to beat about the bush, so let me just repeat that I do not care any more why your friends have such a low opinion of me"—I looked intently into her clear eyes—"but that it *is* of great interest to me, on the other hand, to know why Joachim Stiller is drawn into this conversation. What do you know about him? Where did you get the idea of looking for any connection between me and that peculiar fellow?" Silent, and evidently relieved, she took a folder from the tidily arranged writing desk under the window in the slanting ceiling and handed me a letter. With a shock that caused a pain in the back of my head and neck, I identified the handwriting which from now on I would recognize out of a thousand others. Simone destroyed the letter later, I believe, in a fit of depression, but in outline the content boiled down to this, that it had come to the notice of the sender that the founders of a new magazine were intending for no reason at all to discredit their older colleague, Freek Groenevelt, and that Stiller advised them to abandon this useless plan, since a task was awaiting the person involved that would require the complete application of all his mental and emotional powers.

"Quite frankly, I have the impression," I suggested, "that the writer of this letter belongs to your acquaintances rather than to mine. But anyway, I am completely baffled by this whole crazy affair."

"We were baffled too, Mr. Groenevelt. In the beginning, at least. This letter arrived a few days after the first number was compiled ... I remember there was some postage due on it because it had an invalid stamp."

"Have you kept the envelope?"

"No. Why should I?"

"Please forgive me, but where did you get the notion that I was involved in all this?"

She did not look for some excuse.

"Once the boys are on their pet subject there is no stopping them, you see. Even when the idea of the magazine was still in the air, they really used to run you down dreadfully. I understood that you had written an unjust article about a couple of young poets or something of that nature. And they intended to retaliate."

"Il faut que jeunesse se passe," I smiled disdainfully.

"Some time later the letter arrived. In the meantime the editorial staff had been finally selected. God, how childish it all sounds, looking back ... Suddenly they all seemed to agree that one of the boys who had not gotten what he thought he had a right to, had gone to you to tip you off."

"And then your friends came to the conclusion that I would have received such a tattletale, and besides, would have taken the trouble to write you, under a pseudonym, a kind of begging letter. And this was considered to be more than enough reason to abuse me as if I was the scum of the earth. All in all a fine story—silly as it is!"

I really ought to have laughed out loud, as in a bad play. But I felt it to be a humiliating situation, something like the vomit of strangers that clung to me. I was furious with myself for having listened to Andreas, even for one moment. My hostess confined herself to nodding assent to my supposition. Was she on the verge of tears, or did I imagine it? She said dazedly:

"You don't think that I wrote the article, do you?..."

"There is no sense in talking about it any longer," I replied more quietly. "I am fed up with the whole business, you know. You didn't believe in that story, did you?"

Distracted, she smoothed her skirt over her knees.

"After all, I didn't know you..."

I produced the envelope of my Stiller letter.

"It goes without saying that you are loyal to the others. But do I really look as if I would carry this charlatanism so far as to write letters to myself? I am sure that, as a pedagogue, you will not doubt the identity of the handwriting."

That "pedagogue" was mean, but I had said it before I realized it.

"Heavens, no," she replied, looking more closely at the envelope in confusion. "And it is exactly the same stamp. But then that article was a scandalous piece of injustice, Mr. Groenevelt..."

"Let us call it frivolity. For I am absolutely convinced that you have never read a letter of my work, apart perhaps from an article in the paper. In your eyes I am an old-fashioned fool. If you don't mind, I would like to send you a few of my books. Then you can make up your own mind if I really am the virtual imbecile the *Atomium* louts take me for. I had better go now. Good evening."

I had the impression that she wanted to keep me, but could not find a suitable pretext to do so. She was really upset. Nevertheless, she was firm and clear in everything—that I realized already—and not calculating in any respect.

"I am very sorry," she said dully, after I had formally taken my leave once again, my "good evening" of a moment ago already forgotten. "I really cannot tell you how terribly sorry I am about all this horrible business. Only now do I realize how mean..."

"Let us forget it. It is not the first time something like this has happened to me," I answered lightheartedly. "I should not have been so foolish as to trouble you. Please forgive me..."

Defiantly I let my car accelerate in second gear with a whining roar. Perhaps I would have felt cheerful if this cursed Joachim Stiller, whom I had begun to imagine as a little old gentleman with the beard of Leopold II, had not existed. But it was not even just that, I thought angrily. However, I did not want to admit to myself what in fact was the matter...

CHAPTER 6

Wiebrand Zijlstra's Enterprise

No one would believe me if I asserted that, while writing down these reminiscences from the most confusing period of my life, I never asked myself why I was committing all this to paper. I was obsessed by the thought that I had been involved, if only on the periphery, in a concurrence of events so improbable, yet at the same time so inexplicable and consequently for the outsider not even startling, that I regard it as my duty to put my experiences down in writing. Perhaps it is an illusion, but I do not think it impossible that some time these pages will be added to some scientific file or other when, sooner or later, scholars come to the conclusion—the attitude of exceptionally elevated minds with as much philosophical as poetic and metaphysical sensitivity points more or less in that direction—that science has greater possibilities, even more bafffling than the chemical processes in infernal nuclear reactors or the in-human conjuring tricks of cybernetics; I do not rate them any higher than the punched paper rolls, from the Charleston to the Light Cavalry Overture, that were put in jingling electric pianos when I was a child.

However, I do not wish to digress. I have already noted that my experiences belong in a border area, a no-man's-land so to speak, where mysterious distress signals reached me whose innermost meaning I shall never comprehend. That is why up to now I did not dare make a sharp distinction between the absolute and unmis-takable handwriting on the wall, between the unpronounced, yet no less horrifying, "mene tekel" and certain other events which I witnessed around the same time and in which I even played a part. These had perhaps no connection with the former, yet they were full of such astonishing absurdity that I repeatedly asked myself if they had perhaps been echoes, on the more mundane level of phe-nomena, whose ominous ripples I had felt drawing past me, as on a windless day the walker along the quiet beach is surprised by a sudden stirring of the waves, caused, on closer inspection, by a distant storm or an underwater current.

But all this sounds far too bombastic as an introduction to the story of Wiebrand Zijlstra's reappearance in my life, after I had lost sight of him for many years. Was it an accident or an act of fate? It still surprises me how many detours have sometimes been necessary for one vague and perhaps even wrongly interpreted sign to reach me...

It was a sweltering afternoon and I was sitting on a small terrace on the Oude Vaar Square. It was very quiet and I felt depressed and bored, partly through the influence of the heavy atmosphere and the veiled sun which did not succeed in breaking through the thin cloud cover. Since, in such circumstances, one's glance tends to seek a point of rest, I was gazing thoughtlessly at a monumental urinal that was placed in the middle of the wide road. After a while I began to consider the question of how I could poke fun, in one of my columns, at these indispensable but strange ornaments of the public thoroughfare which, like so many of the less useful monuments in my mother city, are distinguished by a rather belated preference for the Baroque, giving rein in this case to twisted wrought-iron festoons, flourishes, rosettes, and foliage crowned by three mighty gas lamps. I had already watched many passers-by enter this place of introspection to make a libation to the limitation of the human condition, when I spotted Wiebrand Zijlstra.

He wore a smart light-gray summer suit of Italian cut and even at a distance I recognized him immediately from his dancing way of walking. Since the time we had left school together, he had swum through queer and often troubled waters. For a few years he had been a clerk in a stockbroker's office, had run a betting machine at the horse races for a while, and then suddenly had begun studying art history and archeology. During the German occupation some claimed that he worked for the Intelligence Service, while others asserted that he maintained peculiar relations with the local Occupation Headquarters. With a man like him, the one did not exclude the other. He had, however, no difficulties after the Liberation and even before the end of the hostilities I met him in American uniform as a member of a committee concerned with tracing confiscated art treasures. Since then I had lost sight of him.

I heard accidentally that he had gone to Paris and was said to be earning a lot of money in the picture trade on the Left Bank. It did not seem impossible to me. In any case, he looked well-groomed and prosperous. If I had been told that he made his living by doing a bit of drug peddling or by disposing of a couple of white slaves from time to time, I would not have been surprised either. I never felt great sympathy for him but he, on the other hand, as happens sometimes, always showed great affection for me.

Anyway, I did not enjoy the thought of meeting Wiebrand Zijlstra, even if it were only because it was so terribly hot and I, a lone wolf by nature, would not appreciate his fatiguing, extrovert manner. But I thought it childish to hide behind a paper or to walk away, pretending I had not seen him, so I waited, resigned, for the moment when he would bear down on me with expansive gestures, enthusiastically expressing his feelings of friendship.

When only a small distance separated us—he still had not noticed me, although I do not know anyone more observant than he—he hesitated a moment and then walked in the direction of the ornate structure. A moment later I could only see his legs and the back of his head and I hoped with all my heart that the interruption of his walk would divert his attention from his surroundings long enough to make him walk absentmindedly past my little terrace. I concentrated on filling my pipe since a certain shame stopped me from continuing to watch Wiebrand Zijlstra who, for the moment, was confined to helplessness. I had already lit my pipe but he had still not reappeared. To my surprise I noticed how he seemed to be dawdling at leisure around the small circular enclosure and did not make any preparations to continue on his way. I knew his morbid curiosity for all phenomena of life, but this seemed a bit much.

At last he reappeared again, grinning with satisfaction. He stood on the spot where other visitors to the impressive piece of architecture usually check if their pants are zipped up and button up their jacket, and surveyed his surroundings like Bonaparte the battlefield of Austerlitz. He only lacked the right hand in the opening of the jacket. There was to be no escape, I knew that now. His broad grin—he still had those splendid murderous teeth—proved immediately that I had not been wrong; enthusiastically he came up to me, squeezed both my hands exuberantly, rejoiced noisily in our meeting again and called me his very best friend. I underwent this ceremony with resignation but also with a slight physical revulsion, even though I was not altogether immune to his irresistible charm which before, in our schooldays, had made it impossible for me to prevent him from cribbing from me all the time; then I grinned in spite of myself and said with a nod in the direction of the urinal, "Well, I must say you take your time..."

He laughed out loud as though he thought it a marvelous joke and ordered two beers without asking me. "He has aged," I thought to myself, "but in the eyes of a teenage girl or a very young, inexperienced woman, it must give him the somewhat mysterious charm of the gentleman with slightly graying hair." His eyes shining with pleasure, he said: "I can imagine that it must be a complete mystery to you. Really, I haven't become a dirty old man in these few years. But you won't be able to believe your ears when I tell you what it's all about. But no, if I only tell you, you'll think I'm crazy. Come on..." Protesting would do no good. When Zijlstra got something, no matter what, into his head, he carried it through whatever happened. He would have his way, however much one resisted. I was agreeably surprised that he was willing to accept my view that the situation was rather strange.

"With the two of us, it would really look rather peculiar," he said. "I'll wait for you. Just imagine that you want to go urgently and in the meantime, use your eyes!"

"Idiot," I said angrily, but obeyed his command without further useless protest while he quoted something about "not to reason why."

In the meantime he stood outside, whistling a theme from the Pastoral Symphony. I wondered if he wanted to make a complete fool of me, thinking that by somewhat similar means drivers used to make their horses do in appropriate places what elsewhere could have provoked the intervention of some zealous policeman, even though horses are permitted more than people.

"Well, and?" he asked, glowing with enthusiasm.

"Go and fool someone else," I grinned wanly. "If it is a joke, please tell me what you mean. I shall do my best to laugh, if that pleases you!"

"Have you really not noticed anything? Did nothing peculiar strike you?"

"I have seen a filthy wall on which some sex maniac has drawn rather dirty pictures. Is that what you mean?"

"Exactly," he answered, satisfied. "Come, let's have another beer."

He had actually made me curious; one could expect anything from him. Perhaps he had begun studying psychiatry one day and was now involved in some research into certain psychopathic deviations. The strange thing was that I could not only imagine him completing such a task with success, but also writing a widely praised definitive work about it with a bombastic title.

I said noncommittally, "I wonder what you are up to now, Zijlstra. You are the strangest fellow I have ever met. Sometimes I really believe you are slightly off your head..."

"You are not the first to wonder," he said in a tone of voice as if I had paid him a compliment. "But don't judge too hastily. I suppose that, as a journalist, you have a properly trained visual memory, have you?"

"I have never asked myself."

"Anyway, just try to call those pictures you have seen to mind again—yes?"

"I am doing my best, but it is a crazy business."

"Well, in that case I, Wiebrand Zijlstra, shall tell you something. Remember my words. The man who has drawn them is perhaps a sex maniac, as you so mercilessly put it, agreed. But he is also a genius!"

Suddenly I realized that he was not joking at all. At times he could be witty and often it was his sense of humor that silenced his opponents whenever he wanted to make them enthusiastic for some reckless enterprise which would, however, rarely be dangerous to himself. But I knew that he was serious this time, yes, I even had a premonition of what he was about to confide in me. This too was one of the peculiar features in the character of this born adventurer: he possessed a bewildering sincerity, was always straightforward in his own way, never reciprocated the suspicion shown toward him, and when he asserted that he was an open book and had secrets from no one, it really was the precise truth, though nobody could ever make head or tail of him. I assumed an attitude of wait-and-see without concealing the fact—and he would never take offense at that—that his faith in me did not please me at all.

"You must spare me half an hour, Freek," he said with an imploring note in his voice as if his life depended on it. "I know that you're very busy, but an old friend is worth half an hour to you, I hope? I'm going to tell you this in absolute confidence. Later I may call upon you as a journalist, but for the time being I ask you to be silent. You're not a gossip, I know that, of course..."

"Don't worry," I said. "I am as silent as the grave, you can count on that."

"You know that I've only recently come back from Paris..."

"I did not know, but that is probably not important, is it?"

"Perhaps you've heard that I've had quite a good career in the picture trade over there. It is no secret that at the moment I've about a dozen artists practically eating out of my hand, so to speak."

"Or you out of theirs?"

"That's all the same; it is only a question of dialectics. Anyway, after years of experience I came to the conclusion that it was high time I started looking for new blood again. I returned to Antwerp especially to discover new talent. My journey turned out to be a disappointment, to start with, at least. The boys here paint exactly the same as those from Paris—only they usually know their job better. There would be something to do for two or three of them over there, but that isn't enough for me by a long way. After all, I have to cover my expenses, don't I?"

"Of course," I said, "you must definitely cover your expenses."

"You're laughing at me. But that doesn't matter. The day before I decided to clear out again with a few of the local boys' little pieces in my suitcase, exactly the day before, as though heaven had taken pity on me, I urgently wanted to go to the toilet..."

"What for heaven's sake has that got to do with it...But anyway, it happens in the best of families."

"Very well. So I went into a little café, somewhere in the neighborhood of the Horsemarket. There I found, for the first time, that the man I had been looking for in fact does exist."

"Splendid. So everything is fine?"

"Nothing is fine, my dear boy. In fact I only found a few scrawls on the plastered wall of the toilet behind the small bar. But I realized immediately, Freek, that a genius had crossed my path."

"And that genius of yours is the same dirty fellow who...?"

"Yes, call him what you like. That afternoon I went around all the pubs in the neighborhood. Only in a few places had my man left, maybe an obscene but at the same time an amazingly clever drawing. I bought a miniature camera with a flashlight to be able to photograph everything I found immediately. I've already been following his trail stubbornly for weeks. Look for yourself..."

He produced a plan of the city and opened it carefully on the metal pub table. He suddenly made me think of General Rommel in his time. He had marked the plan here and there with red crosses, sometimes a long way from each other and in other places so close that they could hardly be distinguished. I remembered the pins with colored heads which my father used to stick on the map of Russia during the war to follow the progress of the front line.

"Sooner or later I'll catch him," Wiebrand went on, "even if I have to wait a year. In the meantime I've compiled a splendid collection of photographs. You really ought to come and look at them in my hotel. If need be, I could write a thesis about him with the material I have."

"Well, why shouldn't you? I think it really is rather original, you know..."

His story did fascinate me. I ought to have known beforehand. One does not pass by Wiebrand Zijlstra with indifference. What was it he lacked, I wondered, that he was not a great man in his field?

"Perhaps I shall do it in the end," he said dreamily. "But you see, Freek, I want to get that fellow personally, to wake him up, to make him aware of the genius that he is throwing away at the moment. After the war a grocer in Paris in a few years earned a fortune with things that were much worse. I can help that fellow, you see, and—I admit it readily—put aside a nice bit myself after a while. A man has got to live after all, don't you agree?"

"How, do you imagine, are you going to dispose of your graffiti from café toilets and public urinals?"

"That's exactly why I must find him, cost what it may. First I engaged a private detective, but he was a bungler, only accustomed to following illicit couples and spoiling their pleasure. He thought I was crazy and presented me with huge expense accounts, as if my money grew on trees. Then I got the idea of trailing that sleuth himself and I found out that he simply hung around the pubs all day. So I've taken the bull by the horns. I *must* find my man. I want to make a contract with him, with a lawyer if need be, rent a studio, buy him canvas, brushes and paint, place him under the tuition of an engraver or a lithographer for a while, give him pocket money if necessary—anyway, we shall see..."

"Are you sure you are not in danger of making a bad mistake? Do you remember the time when it was the height of fashion to gush over drawings of toddlers or lunatics?"

"I'm sure that I am right. It's a certainty that I feel here, you see," he said, and dramatically indicated the region of his heart. "Are you not struck then, my dear fellow, not struck by the over-powering strength of these scrawls, their precipitous symbolism, their ominous, yawning depth and the nameless fear that dominates our modern world order?"

"No," I answered truthfully, "I have not noticed anything. But since you mention it... I know avant-garde boys who don't produce anything better, but who are nevertheless highly praised."

"I agree," he said, "I agree..." but I could feel that he had listened with only half an ear and was staring at something over my shoulder. "Damn it, Groenevelt," he went on tensely with a voice that trembled suddenly, "damn it, perhaps you have brought me luck..."

I turned round, curious to see what had affected him so suddenly. A gray, completely nondescript little man had come out of the urinal, of no definite age, although I took him to be about forty and got the impression that he was a little backward. He wore a crumpled blue linen pair of pants, a faded jacket that many years ago had belonged to a more solid predecessor, worn-out shoes, a drab beret, and a shabby pair of metal-framed glasses from behind which he looked quickly, but evidently by accident, in our direction. He carried a canvas bag on a leather belt over his shoulders; it was full of papers and far too heavy for his slender frame.

"Do you really think that...?" I hesitated, not quite sure whether Zijlstra was putting on an act in order to impress me—a thing he used to do at school sometimes.

"I'm convinced," he replied, suddenly whispering hoarsely and nearly panting with tension. "I've been watching him quite by accident. He has been inside much longer than is necessary for..."

"Who knows? Perhaps he too is in the picture trade," I suggested feebly, but my companion imperturbably ignored my attempt to be funny.

"Would you mind paying the bill?" he said. "I'll phone you tomorrow. Excuse me..."

Filled with a deep feeling of diffidence that was difficult to describe, I could not bring myself to watch my former school friend leave. I had to admit that his story had fascinated me and, knowing his almost infallible intuition for such things, I was suddenly convinced that he was right. Although I was not insensitive to the obscure humor of the affair, a painful feeling of uneasiness stole over me for which I knew no name, except that of revulsion.

CHAPTER 7

Geert Molijn's Secondhand Bookshop

After I had paid for the beers Zijlstra had treated me to, I trudged off in the direction of home. The time of great unease had not yet come for me. No, I could not say that I felt really depressed, but meeting the art dealer had made me feel uncomfortable all the same. There was something unpleasant in the story he had dished up and this had considerably worsened the feeling of dejection that had already filled me all day. When I heard thunder rumbling in the distance I realized that the weather too had something to do with the fact that I did not feel at ease inside my own skin. It appeared now that the sky was much more overcast than it had been a while ago when one could still hope to see the sun break through at any moment. In the Korte Gasthuis Street the first drops of rain splashed down onto the warm cobbles, and sprinkled five-frank pieces which at first dried up as you watched them. But I had hardly turned into the Lombaardevest when the shower came down like a billowing, rustling curtain. I began to run and, keeping close to the front of the houses, was just able to reach the secondhand bookshop of Geert Molijn before getting soaked. The lively little man who, with his open face, ruddy complexion, and thin tufts of hair, reminded me every time I saw him of a little clown in one of Tytgat's pictures, welcomed me warmly as though I had come especially to make a friendly visit and had not just taken the convenient opportunity of finding shelter from the bad weather in his shop. It was certainly a strange coincidence that it should be him of all people I ended up with after my meeting with Zijlstra. It is difficult to imagine more extreme opposites than these two extraordinary characters. If the presence of the first made me nervous, the company of the second filled me with a pleasant calm and a feeling of trust; it seemed as if the hurried everyday life had no hold over him and came to a halt as soon as one stepped over the threshold of his dark little shop where now, as the thunderstorm was raging with full force, one could hardly distinguish anything. In the winter especially I often dropped in on him at night in his dilapidated house, the last in a bombed-out row, and—I do not really know why—I loved it best when there was a sharp frost or when there had been a fall of snow. Mostly silent, we would sit smoking for hours near the blushing potbellied stove, surrounded on all sides by dusty-smelling books piled high on shelves that reached the ceiling, so that there was hardly any room left for our chairs.

I would be indulging in a rather unjustified generalization if I described Geert Molijn as the traditional wise, old man. For example, I have never regarded his interest in the occult sciences—to call it by a rather vague and general name—and anything else that could possibly be connected with it in any way, including theories about the favorable influence of eating raw food, as an exactly convincing expression of wisdom. To be honest, however, I must add that I am by nature allergic to such things and this would naturally stand in the way of an objective and understanding attitude. What drew me to him especially was the presence of "the milk of human kindness" in everything he did—something that is getting more and more rare in our rationalized society. But it is strange that I hardly knew anything about this good old friend of mine. It was only after a considerable time that I was able to make an approximate reconstruction of some of the important events in his life: that he had been a nationalistic activist in the First World War and that he had lost his post at the State Archives Office as a result of this; that afterwards, since it had become reactionary, he had turned his back on the militant Flemish cause in favor of Trotskyism, that his wife had died in childbirth and that, twenty years later, his son who was a member of the Resistance had died in a German concentration camp. He himself had never told me any details, but I did not regard this in any way as signifying a lack of trust in me. For he was modesty itself, this man whom I had never known to be melancholy, and his sense of propriety, which he sometimes carried to extremes, kept him from talking about himself.

"Can I help you in any way?" he asked; the thought did not even enter his head that there might be a connection between the rainstorm and my appearance.

"To be quite frank, I have only come inside to escape from the rain," I replied honestly. "But if you have got anything special, I would like to have a look at it. I can't buy anything unless you give me credit till the first of next month."

"That'll be all right...I don't really know if it amounts to anything," he said and indicated an untidy pile in the corner. "They're all things I've been able to save from the pulp mill at the very last moment..."

After he had lit the lamp I settled down on the floor. The thunder rolled over the city like an artillery bombardment, with treacherous crashes and long rumbling echoes, while the rain, sometimes interspersed with hail, clattered against the shop window.

"I bumped into Wiebrand Zijlstra this afternoon," I said over my shoulder. "Do you know him?"

"I know him," he mumbled thoughtfully. "He is not a good man..."

I confined myself to an absentminded "Do you think so?" without asking him what he meant precisely.

In the meantime I picked up the books one by one and inspected them perfunctorily; they were mostly grubby and seemed to have been in a cellar for years, since an oppressive smell of damp and mildew emanated from them. They were nothing much, although it surprised me that Molijn had once again laid hands on a pile of writings which were all in some way connected with the many things between heaven and earth to which Horatio's attention once had been drawn. There were pamphlets about telepathy, spiritualism, clairvoyance, levitation, and suchlike hocus-pocus. Among them I found a crumpled volume, spattered with rust spots, from the collected writings of the notorious Madame Blavatsky, as well as a few booklets about astrology and even common or garden conjuring tricks. Just as I was about to lose interest and call a halt, my slackening attention was drawn to a stout octavo volume bound in leather, whose antiquity I noticed immediately. I am no bibliophile, but I possess an intuitive feeling for the atmosphere of a book, old or new—that is to say, I usually know at first glance if it is worthwhile taking a closer look at it.

"Oh yes," the shopkeeper said, "I ought to have put that one aside right away. It seems quite interesting but the title page is missing. I don't know what it is called, who the author is, or when it was published. For the rest it's in quite good condition."

"Sixteenth century," I said, "what do you think?"

"Perhaps the beginning of the seventeenth, but you may be right. It was probably printed in Antwerp. I haven't yet had time to take a serious look at it. You would probably find out in the City Library or the Plantin Museum. I don't know what the thing is worth commercially."

"Would it provide any material for a newspaper article? It is also a slack time from the literary point of view..."

"No idea, but do take it with you. I'll get it back when you have finished with it..."

While the old man went to look for a sheet of newspaper in the dark little room behind the shop, the letter from Joachim Stiller suddenly leapt into my mind. Perhaps it was because of the penetrating smell of old paper which has always slightly nauseated me, but it had also something to do with the fact that Geert Molijn had often been of help to me with his phenomenal memory.

"Listen a moment," I said, "I would like to ask you something. You know more about such things than I do. I have in my possession a handwritten document that I find particularly intriguing. But I do not have the most important factor on which the significance of the whole thing depends. I mean, I don't know when it was written—a few days, or perhaps forty years ago..."

"Child's play," he answered. "Any serious graphologist can give you a moderately accurate date just by looking at the style of the writing..."

"Of course," I interrupted him, "I thought of a graphologist too, but..."

"If you don't find that sufficient, you must take it to Professor Schoenmakers."

"You mean the director of the Antiquarian Research Laboratories?"

"Yes. I was at the university with him. Ring him, give him my regards, and he will do everything possible to help you."

Suddenly the feeling came over me that I had exposed my vulnerable spot to no purpose. It irritated me that I had given in like a weakling to an impulse which I had been able to repress for days, since my encounter with Simone Marijnissen. When I had said good-bye to Molijn and felt the pleasant relief of the cool city, washed clean by the rain, I was filled with the determination not to undertake anything that could make me look ridiculous in my own eyes and even less in those of Professor Schoenmakers, an eminent figure in scholarly circles. I no longer understood how I could have become so worked up about the meeting with Wiebrand Zijlstra and his nonsensical story which probably did not contain a grain of truth. All at once I felt better, had a sandwich and a cup of coffee in a small snack bar on the Suikerrui, and went home with the intention of keeping myself fully occupied all evening with the book my good friend had entrusted to me.

It was hardly light literature, but at the same time I was fascinated by the copious, yet compact, prose of the unknown author whose aim, it appeared, was the analysis and explanation of the Revelation of St. John. It turned out to be the writing of some German mystic translated into the graphic, yet somewhat tortuous, Dutch of the Renaissance. I had the feeling that this strange, sometimes horrifying, and frequently sibylline text, no less sibylline in many places than the Apocalypse itself, badly needed illustrations by Dürer or Urs Graf, while Hiëronymus Bosch also crossed my mind. I am of course no specialist in such matters and I had no way of knowing if the exegesis of John's vision on Patmos presented here deviated to any notable extent from the explanations that were popular in the later Middle Ages, the Age of Humanism, and the Reformation. So as to be able to follow the author step by step I took care to keep the Bible close at hand. I certainly do not deny that through lack of theological and historical training certain fragments were for the present beyond my comprehension. Or was I looking for reason where so-called inspired muddleheadedness had the upper hand? Yet in other places the obsession with destruction, damnation, and death gaped at me in all its horror from the neatly printed pages with such a fascinating power of expression that it had the ring of a magic spell and there seemed to me no doubt of the author's sincerity.

The great multitude, the seven Angels, the woman and the dragon, the beast from the earth, the battle of Michael, the woman sitting upon the scarlet beast, the fall of Babylon and the Last Judgment were to me horrifying phenomena, when they were unwrapped from the archaic and to a certain extent reassuring biblical text which, after all, ends with the vision of the new heaven, the new earth, and the new Jerusalem where the golden streets will be clear as glass. But my sixteenth-century hypochondriac hardly took these last pages into account; he regarded the destruction of all that exists as an unmistakable prophecy. On the contrary, if I understood him rightly—and perhaps he had good reason not to make himself too clear on this point—he questioned the credibility of St. John's encouraging last chapters. To a modern theologian this hybrid hotchpotch could not have been much more than a historical curiosity, the more so since I remembered that some specialist in the field now doubted the validity of interpreting the Apocalypse as the prophecy of the approaching end of the world.

I am not ashamed to admit that my attention gradually slackened while I was reading, until I finally arrived at the concluding arguments of my melancholy guide. As had already become apparent from the preceding pages, these boiled down to the statement that the cosmos in its present form is doomed to destruction, a destruction so absolute that it will again approach the darkness that ruled before the first day of Creation. More and more I got the feeling that the argument of the unknown author differed from his contemporaries' popular interpretation of the vision on Patmos, even if only in that my visionary ignored the appearances of the Lamb as though they meant no more—to put it very irreverently—than a plaster on a wooden leg. Anyway, he must have been a rather unorthodox thinker: obviously the child of a confused age. I thought of the numerous heresies, regarded both from the Lutheran and Roman Catholic points of view, that had flourished so fiercely in Germany in the second half of the sixteenth century, one prophesying the advent of the kingdom of God on earth, the other the complete destruction of all existence. Whereas I had read the book purely out of antiquarian interest and out of my professional curiosity as a journalist one idea, however, only casually touched upon by the author but quite clearly stated, made me shiver—namely the idea that the destruction of creation would take place because of the cessation of time. It was a strange concept which I myself had played with when I was a small boy: what would happen if suddenly time no longer existed? Even my father, who usually understood everything about the child that I was, laughed at it without seeing any precocious profundity in it and reassured me that, if this happened, all clocks in the world would be silent. Years later it still made me feel uncomfortable if the clock on the mantelpiece went wrong and no longer filled the living room with its old familiar ticking.

Meanwhile I reflected ironically that prophets of doom usually have enough sense to take their leave of this worldly vale of tears before their prophecies could come true. That is why I valued the fact that mine did not shirk this difficulty. He painstakingly specified that the cosmos would be reduced to absolute nothingness at the moment when Mars was in the death house of the quadrant of Uranus, the last planet in its turn being in the sign of Leo. Mars would furthermore be in opposition to Jupiter, which would at that moment be in the sign of Scorpio where Neptune would also be found, and the moon would be in the second house of the quadrant of Saturn and also in the trigon of Mars and the sextile of Uranus.

"You don't say," I thought to myself, feeling respect for this painstaking accuracy in spite of myself, even though the complicated astrological terms were pure Chinese to me. I therefore made up my mind to ask a colleague who knew about these things. However, it was to be some time before I carried out this intention.

CHAPTER 8

A Night Out

Around midnight, when I was just about to go to bed, pretty tired from reading the book that was as confusing as it was pessimistic, the front-door bell rang. Irritated, I put on a coarse woolen sweater which I only wear indoors and hurried downstairs. Although there was no reason for alarm I felt relieved when I recognized Andreas, accompanied by my publisher Dirk Boersma and his wife Eveline who were on their way from Florence to Amsterdam. The excellent mood all three of them were in was unmistakably due to a well-lubricated meal in one of the Chinese, Greek, Armenian, or Yugoslav restaurants which flourish in the dock area. Andreas especially was rather tipsy, which was obvious from the fact that he greeted me joyfully in French. When he has had a few, he always starts speaking French.

"Mon cher," he said, "mon cher, you don't know how pleased we are that we have found you at last."

"We phoned you three times before we went to have a meal," added Boersma, "but we got no answer. In the end, we had to give up..."

"Come in—or won't you be content with a flask of old gin?"

"No, you old rascal," Andreas decreed, making a visible effort to keep his words under control, "we have come to pick you up. The publishing trade is paying—that much it owes us in any case!"

I suggested that they should come upstairs anyway to have a drink while I changed into something else. But Eveline thought I looked very nice in my coarse sweater and maintained that I really did not need to smarten myself up. She linked arms with Andreas and me and we agreed to buy a pick-me-up in one of the cafés of the Stadswaag. She gave little shrieks of delight when we arrived at the seventeenth-century square which for years had been the center of a curious kind of night life—curious, because it appeared largely devoid of the reddish glow I find so unpleasant and which is cus-

55

tomary elsewhere. Basically I am a puritan. The Stadswaag, however, does not evoke a Calvinistic repugnance in me even if the young people who hang around there imagine they rival the fauna of Saint Germain des Prés.

First of all we had a brandy in the "Pimpernel" and after that, as we climbed up the steep ladder to the "Flying Dutchman," right up in the attic, Eveline's enthusiasm knew no bounds. She is a nice, strapping wench, baked from solid Dutch clay, and there is an amusing contrast between her robust Batavian health and the bohemian airs she had acquired through mixing with the poets whose work her husband published. The "Flying Dutchman" was decorated with fish nets, cables, storm lanterns, life belts, pieces of cork, and other nautical requisites while, purely for esthetic effect, a cosy fire burned brightly in the open fireplace and sent out a tropical heat; for this reason we preferred to drink beer which after a while made a treacherous alliance with the brandy we had hardly assimilated. I noticed with pleasure how the drunkenness rose in me and thought this night's outing an excellent ending to a rather depressing day. Although I am a lone wolf by nature I sometimes feel a sudden need for the company of good friends. Andreas and Dirk Boersma were having an earnest discussion about the state of Dutch literature, while Eveline cast melting glances in my direction; these were mainly due to the percentage of alcohol in her healthy peasant blood and the reflection of the dancing candle-lights in her somewhat too large eyes.

"Damn it," Andreas said, "it's awful warm here. I'm just about bursting with the heat. Shall we go somewhere else and have a good strong cup of coffee?"

Once past a certain point, Andreas called everything he drank coffee. However, I cannot remember ever having seen him partake of coffee in these circumstances. He and Dirk stumbled down the perilous staircase with difficulty, but I was still able to offer my arm chivalrously to Eveline although I searched in vain for the appropriate quotation from *Faust*.

I guided them to the "Monks' Cellar" where the beer is very good and where it is usually rather quiet around this time. My three friends were more than enough for me, and even though it was unlikely that there would be any more coherent conversation I still preferred their companionship to the flirting or the noise of amorous or rowdy teenagers in most of the bars in the neighborhood. But on the other hand I did not think it at all necessary to resort to one of the more select spots like the "Nemrod," the "Tanchelmus" or the "Venushof." When we entered the gothic "Monnikenkelder" (which was actually the last remnant of a medieval abbey and had not been desecrated by its new function because it clearly revealed the architecture of a wine cellar) it appeared that I had been mistaken. Apart from the handful of regular midnight customers who practically live there, a noisy group had also pitched camp; at first sight they seemed to be making a night of it after some official party or other. At the top of their voices they encouraged the small band that normally confined itself after midnight to playing sleepy tunes, and occupied the dance floor uninterruptedly, to the annoyance of two amorous couples under high voltage who were not able, so to speak, to dance into seventh heaven, and this the vampire-like "lady crooner" did in fact assert in German with a Flemish accent.

My companions did not seem to be bothered by the crowd and I had to give Dirk's jacket a tug several times to prevent him from clambering onto a chair and proposing a toast to Belgium and the Benelux. He did not take offence at this and, far too boisterously for my liking, began a discussion about the fact that these mad Belgians made damned good writers; the cause of this was thought to be a more uninhibited way of life which in its turn was due to the fact that ten Catholic priests were not as bad as half a Protestant minister. Partly in French, partly in an imitation of the pinched accent of The Hague that I had never heard from him, Andreas tried to persuade Dirk to double the number of priests in order that they would end up with at least one whole minister, but the publisher thought that this halved man of God was such an excellent invention that he would rather leave the extra ten good shepherds out in the cold without any qualms.

I was acutely conscious of the fact that I was suddenly quite tipsy; I convinced myself that my liver was in perfect working order, that the bile was flowing beautifully into my duodenum, that my kidneys were working like a petrol pump and, in short, that nothing could happen to me. I was never so drunk that I was not aware of wanting to avoid being sick, with all its humiliating consequences. For that reason I decided to take a walk to the toilet, forced to this less by circumstances than by the vague consideration that it was now especially important to keep the bodily functions running smoothly.

I let the cold water run over my wrists and freshened up my face. Then I carefully combed my hair and was just trying to pull my worn sweater straight when I noticed in the mirror before me how the door was opened gingerly and a strikingly well-dressed young woman shyly entered. Even before I could draw her attention to the fact that she had made a mistake and had come into the men's room, I caught my breath, for I suddenly recognized Simone Marijnissen. It also became suddenly clear to me that she belonged to the festive group to which I had so far not paid the slightest attention. To produce the impression that I felt perfectly at ease, I gave a last pull at the collar of my sweater and walked calmly to the exit where she was waiting for me, evidently timid.

"How nice to see you," I smiled, and I meant it, "but I think you have come through the wrong door."

She looked at me intently, and obviously in a hurry.

"You're drunk," she replied. "I had already noticed that you were drunk, but I must still speak to you immediately!"

I made a helpless gesture trying to indicate to her that these surroundings were totally inappropriate for any conversation whatsoever.

"Very well," I mumbled nevertheless, as a giddy feeling overwhelmed me, and I broke out in a cold sweat because I was frightened that I was going to be sick after all. "Very well, but don't you think that..."

"No, not here of course," she answered excitedly. "But when the band plays again you must persuade your friends to dance with a few of my colleagues." I looked most surprised and must have had a rather inane expression on my face. "We are having a night out with the people from the school, the people from the Atheneum, you know. The boss is retiring, and that's why..."

"Anything you say," I grimaced. "Completely at your service!"

"You too must dance with them a couple of times. Then you must ask me without it being very noticeable!" Gradually it dawned on me that this was a well-thought-out strategic plan. "Please do as I say," she went on with a pleading note in her voice. " I really have to speak to you urgently. It is most important..."

There was a sound of approaching steps and even before Dirk Boersma entered with lagging steps, on his guard against the many pitfalls endangering his balance, she had disappeared again. While the publisher, his back turned to me, kept me talking, I collected all the mental reserves I could muster. It was not much but nevertheless I came to the conclusion that a well-educated woman would not run the risk of compromising herself at the entrance to a gentlemen's toilet, unless she had a very good reason. This strenuous thinking had sobered me up somewhat and when a glass of mineral water had woken up my lethargic stomach, I felt excellent. My suggestion of asking the ladies from the other group for a dance was well received. Dirk Boersma intrepidly opened the offensive, stimulated by the thought that there is nothing like a Belgian woman, closely followed by Andreas, who put on a Don Juanesque charm. A neat, elderly Jewish gentleman who had been philosophizing in solitude over a whisky and soda about the Promised Land took pity on Eveline; his head just reached her shoulders. I took my chance with a little teacher wearing American glasses to whom one would have given absolution without confession, but who snuggled up so fondly to me with her entire body (which was not as thin as one would have thought at first sight) that I made an embarrassed grin in Simone's direction. In any case, I admired her strategy. Soon the dance floor was nearly full and even the most jealous lover—assuming she had such a phenomenon—could not have taken offence at my asking her to dance, and even less suspect that we were involved together in a plot. I had the feeling I was succeeding beautifully in putting on a guileless face, just as one does when one talks about sweet nothings while dancing with an unknown lady and without showing too much interest in the conversation.

"Well," I asked, while the trumpet screamed out heartrendingly, "whatever are you worrying about on such a jolly evening?"

Seeming indifferent, she looked over my shoulder, but I could feel her shiver. Suddenly I felt very sorry for her.

"You mustn't think it ridiculous. I don't care about my colleagues, but I wouldn't like the boys from the magazine to notice."

"Good God, I had forgotten all about them. The *Atomium* boys?" She nodded.

"Heavens above," I went on, "surely you're not afraid of them? You're trembling like a leaf..."

"I'd rather they didn't notice, but I am not afraid of them, of course. But I am terribly nervous..."

"Forget about them and come with us. I'll introduce you to my friends. They are really very nice people. A stiff drink will make you feel better and we can still have a lot of fun together. I'll treat you to a bite to eat in a Chinese restaurant. Yes?..."

"I would love to," she answered, "but, you see, my fiancé..."

"Shit," I said from the bottom of my heart, "shit, shit, shit. I bet he is the bastard who has called me everything under the sun in your trashy magazine. But that is not why I say 'shit,' you know, Simone!" I suddenly had the feeling that the moment had come to address her more familiarly. "Was it perhaps to announce your engagement that you...?"

She shook her beautiful head. Her profile made me think of a most exquisite cameo.

"I am so terribly excited because I've had a letter again. A very strange letter. You know, from Joachim Stiller... What in heaven's name does he want from me?"

I felt completely sobered up.

"Give it to me," I said, "now it is really going too far..."

She moved her hand in my back and I heard something like the rustling of paper.

"O.K.," I said, "let's go on playing it discreetly..."

At that moment the dance finished. With the feigned clumsiness of one who has had a few too many I kissed her fingertips. She understood my intention and pushed the letter which she had crumpled up into a ball into my hand. While Eveline, Dirk, and Andreas appeared to be getting on fine with Pedagogy I sat down again at our empty table and smoothed out the document perfunctorily. I was no longer surprised to recognize the scholastic handwriting of Joachim Stiller. But my heart was pounding nonetheless as I read the following message:

Dear Miss Marijnissen, as was to be expected with two people chosen by me, the path of Freek Groenevelt has crossed yours. It was not foreseen that further consequences would follow from this. Yet, on the other hand, nothing can be undertaken lest Free Will lose its rights. Do not fear. What will be, will be. I cannot say yet whether you will be granted a long time for it, although no one knows you both as

thoroughly as I know you. May nothing human be unknown to you.
Your servant, Joachim Stiller.

I took the opportunity, as the band started a new tune, to ask her
to dance once more, but not before I had drunk a glass of dry gin
at the bar. As I led her to the dance floor I felt cheerful as never
before. It left me cold that the greasy young man who apparently
accompanied her, and therefore was probably the fiancé, had been
looking at me suspiciously. I pressed her close to me and said:
"The letter is nonsense, of course. It's a joke of those friends of
yours. The bunglers want to take us in. I can see right through
them, you know!" "Please, speak more softly," she replied anxiously,
and looked at me reprovingly, because I was teasingly playing with
the button of her bra through the back of her dress. "Really, it's not
as simple as you think." "Nonsense," I said with a drunkard's recklessness, "don't take it to heart. They will laugh themselves silly,
if they know that you're taking it to heart. Why should I keep
quiet for such scum? Anyway, they recognized me long ago, of
course, in spite of my old sweater."
I was deliciously drunk again and was floating on a little cloud.
My stomach—good stomach, I thought, and wondered where in
Shakespeare it occurred, excellent stomach—made itself felt only
through an enormous appetite for chicken curry or something like
that. I was sure that I could go on drinking all night and feel better
from hour to hour.
"So far nobody has recognized you ... I could hardly recognize
you myself. Surely, you do not usually wear glasses?"
"Of course not. I only wear glasses to read and work. What has
that got to do with it?"
She laughed openly now; I saw her beautiful teeth and suddenly
it became clear to me that she was the most beautiful woman I
had ever seen. Only then did I realize that I was still wearing
my glasses.
"Good heavens," I grinned, "how did that happen? But damn it,
surely you need not be ashamed of knowing me in front of those
fellows?"
She looked at me shyly, blushing too, but without turning her
eyes away.
"My fiancé is terribly jealous. As a woman, can one blame a

man?...He would not believe that we have met here by accident. He can be very difficult, you know..."

I admit that I took advantage of the fact that I was patently in no condition to behave responsibly when I answered, "Well, it's not human that a nice girl like you is frightened of the first school-teacher that comes along. Will he give you a thousand lines? It's a shame if you ask me. If I were you, I would tell him that he can piss off once and for all. Shall I do it for you?...And here is your letter back. I am sure that it is that loverboy of yours who, out of jealousy, is trying to give you a fright with this garbage, after trying it out on me first." I suddenly became extremely excited, although I did realize that there was something wrong with my reasoning.

"And now, let him get annoyed until he's blue in the face," I concluded defiantly as I led her back to her group, took off my glasses with a flourish, and put them nonchalantly in my trouser pocket.

I saw her stiffen—with fear?—and I was filled with a nameless drunkard's pity. Back with my friends who were enjoying rolls with cheese and mustard, I watched her intently from a distance. The greasy young man appeared to be making a scene, but she apparently did not bother to reply to his excited argument.

"Later on, that aspiring bedroom dictator will take her home," I thought suddenly, with tears in my eyes. "They will take a taxi and on the way he will nag her for quite a while. But afterwards he will come round, because she is living alone and seems to be quite independent. In a couple of hours' time she will perhaps be screaming with rapture and after that they will laugh themselves silly about the trick they have played on me, a trashy writer who is worth nothing to them..."

I knew that it was mean of me to think of her like that. But I was terribly drunk that night and also suddenly terribly alone, as if I did not know how my life should now go on...

CHAPTER 9

A Visit to the Public Library

On leaving the "Monks' Cellar" I said good-bye to my friends. Dirk Boersma kept on stubbornly that he did not want to go to his hotel, damn it all, before he had seen a striptease show, although Eveline was in such a state of spiritual ecstasy that I wondered if she would not like to stage such an exhibition on her own account. But this would of course not be terribly original within the bonds of conjugal union, unless she considered the possibility of acquiring Andreas and me as spectators. At home, I put my finger as far as possible down my throat and puked elaborately with philosophic resignation, after which I drank half a bottle of soda water and swallowed a couple of liver pills. I slept like a log and woke up without a hangover. The cold water of the shower made my skin tingle. Since there was plenty of copy ready at the paper and Clemens Waalwijk, whom I had phoned as a matter of form, assured me that not a single task was waiting for me, I decided to spend the whole day closely studying the book which Geert Molijn had entrusted to me; I wanted to get a detailed and serious article about it ready for our Sunday literary page. I breakfasted elaborately, pleased with my intention to do a lot of work, drank about five cups of coffee, and in a pleasant mood sauntered to the City Library.

It was a morning of sharp contrasts of light, bluish shadows, fruit and flower stalls, the smell of lavender, thin low-necked summer dresses and bare suntanned legs above high heels. Conscience Square, closely hemmed in and dominated by the impressive façade of the Carolus Borromeus Church, in the pollinated light looked like a Venetian piazza, complete with the traditional pigeons, while the statue of our famous writer Hendrik Conscience still sat bent over his aquarium, brooding over what he had done by teaching his people to read Courths Mahler.

The silence in the library filled me with a pleasant feeling. In the almost deathly hush of the reading room where one could hardly hear the rustle of pages being turned, a few girls, obviously student teachers, were industriously copying an encyclopedia, an elderly gentleman turned over the pages of an unmanageably bulky volume of some newspaper, and behind the counter my friend Wim Valckeniers sat dreaming peacefully about the order of the universe. He revived when he saw me and asked enthusiastically how he could be of help to me.

"Listen," I said hesitatingly, "I don't know if I ought to take up your time with a thing like this. It is about a book of which the title page is missing, so that I do not know the title, the author, or the publisher. The text is complete. It was probably printed in Antwerp in the beginning of the seventeenth century, although I am only guessing..."

"Understood," he said. "Have you got it with you?"

I handed him the volume I had been clasping carefully under my arm. In his experienced and yet loving way of opening the book, only a softly smoldering pipe was missing, I thought, and a pair of glasses pushed nonchalantly onto his forehead. At the same time I felt that the modern reading room was far too businesslike for this moment in my private eternity. There ought to have been a dusty study, unpolished windows, and behind them a neglected garden and rain on a red-brick path.

"You are right," Valckeniers muttered, "beginning of the seventeenth... Probably from the workshops of Vostermans, to judge from the layout and the font."

"You are a marvelous librarian," I replied hopefully. "It would be wonderful if I could trace the missing information..."

"Don't overestimate me," he grinned, and it struck me that he still lifted the left corner of his mouth in the same way as he had done more than twenty years ago when we were still at school, which gave his asymmetrical features a comic and likable expression. "But before we enter upon scientific investigation, let us try Fortune... Can you tell me roughly what the book is about? One can find things purely by accident in the most unexpected places."

"The only clue that comes to mind is 'apocalypse,' I think. But I suppose you have got a lot on that..."

I followed him to the silent catalogue room where, after some nimble-fingered searching, he took out a card, noted down the shelf number, and sent a subordinate to fetch the work concerned

from the stacks. I asked no questions for the present. Wim Valckeniers is a very nice fellow, but one has to give him a chance of
displaying a bit of mystery from time to time—a thing not understood by some people who regard such behavior as ambiguous.

He looked triumphant when the library assistant reappeared after
about ten minutes and handed him a volume bound in waxy parch-
ment which, to judge from the outward appearance at least, was
remarkably similar to Geert Molijn's book. Since I did not wish to
spoil his pleasure, I stared dreamily past him on purpose, while
he compared the first page of the text of one book with the other.

"There you are, my dear sir," he exclaimed jubilantly, "a lucky
draw. Look for yourself!" and he pushed the two opened works
toward me over the table.

Had it been really true that a short but deep sleep had sobered
me up completely? Or had I, on the contrary, come blind drunk,
and I mean completely blind drunk, to the library, tottering on my
feet, straight from the "Monks' Cellar" or heaven knows where
else? In any case, the floor suddenly swayed treacherously up and
down, I felt the blood drain away from my face and a queer,
strangled feeling, as if I was going to be sick, enclosed my stomach
and windpipe at the same time, while my heart was thumping so
violently that its beats throbbed against my eardrums, causing a
numb, elastic sensation. I closed my eyes tightly, as if to drive
away a frightening hallucination, but when I opened them again,
concerned mainly with preventing the librarian noticing my consternation which was now growing into panic, I read to my horror
for the second time, my head reeling and my lips muttering in
spite of myself: THE APOCALYPSE, BEING THE VISION OF
ST. JOHN ON PATMOS. EXPLAINED AND ELUCIDATED
BY JOACHIM STILLER, MASTER IN THEOLOGY IN
AUGSBURG.

"And it comes from the press of Vostermans," Valckeniers added
triumphantly, "just as I thought; here is the printer's mark, look
for yourself! But my dear boy, you are very pale!" he went on in the
same breath, "are you not feeling well?"

I really broke out into a sweat now and I could feel it trickling
from my hair over my forehead. Valckeniers fetched a glass of water
which I emptied at one draft while the reading room was still list-
ing terribly as if we were onboard a sinking ship. I held on to the

table so tightly that my knuckles became very white. I vaguely
realized that the student teachers were busily whispering and staring at me stealthily over their encyclopedias. And just as vaguely
did I remember that once before in my life had I known this
almost animal-like fear, right at the end of the war when a rocket
bomb, in a bewildering interval of silence, tore to pieces the trolley
that had just driven off before I could work my way onto the
rear platform. The busy crossroads where it happened was changed
within a fraction of a second into a hecatomb full of splintered
glass, twisted steel, and mutilated bodies. It seemed as if this
terrible memory, which will remain a nightmare to me for the
rest of my life, this time turned out to be my salvation.

"I am in the reading room," I repeated doggedly to myself, "the
incident of the bomb happened a long time ago. Everything here
is peace and safety. There is nothing to be afraid of, nothing can
happen to me..." With the fanaticism of a drowning person who
hopes to reach the shore, I tried to pull myself together, staring at
my white hands. The shadowy figure of Valckeniers stood watching me worriedly out of a sunny haze; he was apparently wondering
if he should call for help.

"Thank you," I whispered hoarsely, "it is getting a bit better...
I really ought to have my blood pressure checked..."

"I thought you were going to faint," I heard him say from far
away, and it sounded even softer than a whisper.

"I got a terrible fright. Are you really feeling better? Would
you like to lie down somewhere quiet?"

I did my best to smile and mumbled with difficulty that it would
be all right. My friend switched on the fans and the cool air did
me good. I could breathe more easily, I had the impression that my
blood began to flow again, and the panic slowly ebbed away, like
the water from the beach at the turning of the tide. Finally I
managed to say in a more or less steady voice:

"Please forgive me, Wim...I am causing you a lot of trouble.
If I had known beforehand..."

"Doesn't matter at all...Shall I walk you home? The boss won't
mind, I'm sure..."

"Really," I answered as decisively as possible, touched by his
sympathy, "I've gotten completely over it now. I am quietly going
to note down the data on the title page and then ferret through

the *Deutsche Bibliographie* and the *Herder*. I am determined to find out what sort of fellow that Mr. Stiller was."

"You stay where you are, old boy, I'll find it for you...," Valckeniers said accommodatingly. Even before I could protest he had sat himself down opposite me with a fat tome. "Well," he said in the same sympathetic tone of voice, "we won't learn much, I'm afraid. But he does seem to have been a peculiar sort of fellow. Both the date of birth and death of our man are unknown. But he did in fact teach theology in Augsburg from 1552 till 1555. That at least agrees with what we know...Expelled from the university because of subversive ideas...Is supposed to have wandered for a while through Bavaria, Westphalia, and the Netherlands as a wayside preacher, but this is not certain. Sounds good, don't you think?... Some identify him with the Stiller, also spelled Stieler, first name unknown and probably of Jewish origin, who was roasted over a slow fire in Geneva in 1560, but that is also supposition. He does not seem to have written anything more than that Apocalypse story of yours..."

It did me good to take down in shorthand the data given to me by my helpful friend. It compelled me to concentrate. I clung to this modest occupation with desperate courage and when I had finished, I felt almost my old self again—physically, I mean. But Wim would not withdraw his fatherly protection so soon. He decided that I needed a drink, that only good old Dutch gin could make my recovery complete, since one has to combat ill with ill. He asked an assistant to take over the supervision of the reading room from him and guided me to a small room on the middle floor where his modest headquarters were situated. Here he conjured up a flask of gin and two glasses from behind an elderly edition of Larousse. "No," he said, "I've not taken to drink. It's the remainder of a present...To your health. You can always have that blood pressure of yours checked. Only, I don't understand how something like that can come up suddenly." "It is completely beyond me," I replied neutrally. "It was the first time..." "It's nerves if you ask me. But be that as it may, you badly need a drink now. Prosit!"

"Prosit!" I replied as cheerfully as I could, and while I drank I realized that it would do me good. "To Joachim Stiller," I added, but I could hear a false note in my bravado. Driven by a sudden need for confidentiality, I went on: "I carried on like a hysterical grandmother, but I couldn't help it. Please forget it..."

"You needn't make any excuses. Nerves, a bit of tension, manager's sickness they call it in America these days, I believe. You ought to take up some innocent hobby, if you ask me: stamp collecting or fishing... Things get the better of me too, sometimes, although it's quiet working here. You ought to start something, something completely unimportant which has no connection at all with your daily work!"

"Not a bad idea..."

"I've been amusing myself lately in this way by meddling in graphology. It's nonsense perhaps, but I can heartily recommend it as a means of relaxation. Have you got a few lines of handwriting on you by any chance?"

The gin had gone slightly to my head, but it did not make me feel sick as on the previous night and the alarming thumping of my heart had by now completely disappeared. I was not drunk and had the impression I could think intensely and sharply again.

"My own hieroglyphics don't interest me," I mumbled as I produced from my wallet the envelope, carefully folded in two, which had contained Stiller's first missive. "But there is a fellow, completely crazy as far as I can see, who is trying to provoke me by sending me idiotic letters. He is even trying to put one over on me with stamps which haven't been valid for a long time. Here, take it..."

"I'm only an amateur, of course. Compared with fellows like Christiaan Sipido who works for the Attorney General, you know, I'm only a toddler from kindergarten. But let me have a look... Do you know this mad correspondent of yours?"

"Not at all. I haven't even the vaguest idea who it may be. It is probably just a joke... Well, Mr. Graphologist, I'm listening!"

"It isn't easy, you know... I really ought to consult my manuals. But anyway... it's quite possible that certain subtleties escape me and it will be precisely those that count, you'll see..."

"Go ahead. I'm not expecting sensational revelations."

"Well, at first sight then, I would hazard a guess that this customer of yours is lacking in personality to a high degree..."

"Which on its own could also be a form of personality, don't you think?"

"If you want to look at it that way...I could be completely wrong, Freek, and I did warn you. But if you insist that I express my opinion as strongly as possible..."

"Don't have any scruples. It is not about an affair of state..."

"Well, in that case I would say that only someone who does not exist, but who can write nonetheless—well, I'm not a literary man—would write in about the same way as your man. It probably isn't very clear, is it?.."

I gulped down my drink and tried to persuade myself that it was the gin that made me shiver so intensely. But deep inside myself I knew that I had shivered because Valckeniers had unwittingly stirred something in me that had been lying dormant for a long time.

· "On the contrary," I mumbled, staring ahead of me, deep in thought, "you cannot possibly realize how disconcertingly you have put it into words...I wonder if it is physically possible that he exists..."

"Strictly speaking, I don't think he does exist," suggested my friend, who naturally couldn't understand what I meant, since I myself did not even know very clearly. "These poor wretches send their letters anonymously, of course, under a false name."

"Yes," I said cheerfully, although the cheerfulness sounded suspiciously unreal, "yes, a false name, that's it, definitely!"

I felt Valckeniers's glance, usually serene, rest upon me inquiringly this time. I pretended not to notice on purpose and stared intently at the faded green backs of the *Larousse du XIX Siècle*, once also the showpiece of my father's modest library. Could I make my old schoolfriend notice that there was a short circuit somewhere inside me....?

CHAPTER 10

Telephone Conversation before Dawn

Although it seemed illogical to me afterwards, I sauntered home in a serene mood. Valckeniers's drink had made me feel a lot better, even though it would have been more in keeping with my character to brood over the crazy coincidence that a sixteenth-century theologian of dubious quality used to have the same name as my enigmatic correspondent. But the certainty that it was a coincidence, that it could not be anything else, was still completely beyond doubt, and this reduced the affair for the present to the proportions of one of the rather unimportant anecdotes that tend to circulate in any editorial office. The only thing that irritated me was the memory of the violence with which I had reacted—almost like a neurotic—to this name that was so sharply familiar to me. I am as fit as a fiddle and do not even know what it is like to be ill. But this is precisely the reason why I do not seem to lack talent for playing the role of "malade imaginaire." Whenever a few cases of polio are reported I no longer feel safe, rarely do I read an article about lung or any other kind of cancer without consequences, and the least little muscle ache in my left arm immediately awakens fears of angina pectoris which last for days. But this time I remained free of all groundless fears, practically certain that there was only something slightly wrong with my blood pressure.

I looked with pleasure at the sunny city scene and remembered with tenderness Simone's excitement of the previous night. I was thinking so intensely of her that I did not dare believe right away that it was in fact she who suddenly stood before me near my house. This encounter apparently surprised her less than me, which was completely logical since it was she who had come to see me—so she told me hurriedly; she had stood before a closed door, had phoned the newspaper in vain from a telephone booth, and, hoping that I would come home around midday, had whiled away the time by looking in shop windows.

70

"You don't know how pleased I am to see you," I said, shaking her fresh, firm hand; I meant it wholeheartedly and immediately produced my key. "Please don't mind the rubbish upstairs," I added, "I happen to be one of those eccentric lone wolves."

She was wearing a marvelous dress with large flowers on a black background and red shoes with high stiletto heels, so sharp that I could not understand how she kept her balance. I appreciated it that she thought it quite natural to come with me without unnecessary ceremony. She belonged to the type of woman that still intimidates me—women who are simple and uninhibited yet show, by the care with which they dress, for example, that they are thoroughly aware of their femininity without affectation or banal coquetry.

"It is lovely here," she said with an elation that contained not a hint of simulated excitement. I was pleased that she enjoyed the atmosphere of my rather extraordinary abode so openly. "And good heavens, Mr. Groenevelt, what a breathtaking view you have here. You must have thought that I lived in a terribly petit-bourgeois place."

"On the contrary," I replied, and joined her by the open window. "I have often thought of the evening we first met. Did you think me very rude that time?"

She laughed with a soft guttural sound that seemed extremely refined to me, and she put her hand on my arm quite naturally, as if to convince me more effectively.

"Not at all, what gave you that idea? But I did get an awful shock when you stood in front of me so unexpectedly. I suddenly realized that I did not have an entirely clear conscience, you see..."

The roofs were shimmering in the afternoon heat and the sky was a greenish blue like the porcelain tops of some old oil lamps. Somewhere deep inside me lived the awareness that nothing else of importance needed to happen to keep the memory of this moment fresh for the rest of my life.

"If I'm not mistaken, we called each other by our Christian names last night," I said. I did not think it right to force Fate to yield more than it wanted to by letting the silence last longer than was strictly necessary. "Shall we agree to continue doing so?"

"If you insist, Mr.—I mean, Freek, I shall do my best. I am really very docile by nature, you know. Anyway, I hope you don't think I am a forward bitch. I don't really understand where I got the impudence to come and visit you so shamelessly."

"Just what I have been asking myself all this time," I joked. "But now that you are here I suggest we have a cup of coffee. There is not a housewife in this city who can make better coffee than I."

While I was busy in the kitchen she continued to admire the panorama; most of my visitors cannot get enough of it. Although I had grossly exaggerated my extraordinary ability to make coffee I had no need to be ashamed of my brew. I left the flask of gin in the refrigerator. Not for all the money in the world would I want her to think that I was a habitual drinker. I did not need to fool myself and I was thoroughly aware that I was far from indifferent to the opinion she must have formed of me by now.

I did not think it necessary to ask questions. On the other hand, it seemed to me that courtesy could hardly require me not to look at her discreetly and with pleasure after we had sat down, she on the couch with her flowery dress spread out around her and I on a little three-legged stool in an expectant but nevertheless patient attitude.

"I could not rest before apologizing for my silly behavior last night," she began without prompting, which did not surprise me. From our first meeting I had known that nothing was as alien to her as artificiality. "I carried on like a teenager..."

"Not a bit of it," I replied seriously, so that she would notice that I did not want to get out of it with a cliché. "You used the opportunity to come to me with your worries, completely spontaneously and without false shame. It all went rather strangely, but that was due to the circumstances. I can imagine how you felt."

"I would have come to you in any case," she went on, smoothing an imaginary crease in her dress. "I dislike ambiguous situations and I had to talk to you. That insane letter thoroughly upset me."

"Try to forget the whole business...Whatever our man Stiller has in mind, I am grateful to him for causing me to see you again."

Perhaps it all started because of the seriousness with which she looked at me with those beautiful eyes of hers, while a great silence one could almost grasp filled the somewhat dusky room. The thought struck me that I would not know what to do with my distress if ever those eyes looked at me reproachfully. In order not to show my confusion I offered her a cigarette. I could see in the way she exhaled the smoke that she wanted to say something, but could not find the right words right away. I understood that I had to help her.

"And now, out with it," I said. "If it is just an ordinary friendly visit, I am more than happy. I cannot say how happy it made me when I realized it was you who suddenly stood before me. If it is just about a business matter, I'd rather you broke my heart without beating around the bush."

"I don't know what you would call a business matter," she replied, smiling with relief. "A while ago I was convinced I had to tell you a lot of things, but now I'm wondering if I ought to trouble you with them."

I refilled her cup and took the opportunity to sit down beside her. "I would appreciate it very much," I said quietly, without showing how touched I was, "if you would consider me as your friend. You are very brave but I can sense that you are upset. I don't know what I can say to reassure you, but you must not forget that the sun is shining gloriously outside, that a little while ago you liked my poor artist's attic and that we are both independent and spiritually mature people who can face whatever problems may come along."

"Forgive me," she said firmly, "I am not in the habit of letting myself go so easily. But I feel pursued; I hardly dare open the mailbox or answer the telephone and in the street I keep looking behind me."

"Good heavens," I said, perplexed, "why didn't you tell me this last night? You merely said that you were nervous. We ought to have left the whole drunken gang and gone to a quiet bar to talk the whole thing over in peace."

"Up till last night it wasn't too bad. I did get upset about those two strange letters, but that was mainly annoyance, not insuperable fear..."

"Even annoyance is going too far, you know... Some joker wants to fool us completely. Believe a journalist, Simone, when he tells you that there are some very strange customers walking around under our Dear Lord's beautiful sun..."

"It isn't just the letters anymore. This morning, when it was hardly light, I was startled by the ringing of the telephone. I was giddy with sleep for I had taken two aspirins. It must have been a long-distance call, I think. An operator got through to me first, but I did not hear her say where the call came from. The aspirins, you see...For a while there was only a humming sound. Then a soft, remarkably cultured man's voice—and it was this particular refinement in his voice that immediately struck me—said that I was speaking to..."

"Why stop so suddenly? I am dying of curiosity!" I said, but I knew what would follow.

"It is too ridiculous for words. But I know I didn't dream it. That unknown voice said that I was talking to Joachim Stiller."

My self-control surprised me. But now that there could be no real doubt in my mind (in spite of a couple of unexplained details) that we were involved in a bad joke, I did not feel any inclination to show even the slightest agitation.

"Well," I muttered lightly, "our little man is persistent enough. What did he want from you so early?"

"I got such a shock that I felt even more dazed, although I was already trembling on my legs. I cannot recall the conversation word for word. I understood what he told me, but not everything he actually said sunk in completely because I was so confused; it boiled down to this—that it had not been very brave of me last night to leave you to your fate, that you felt terribly lonely and sad, that we must never abandon a human being to loneliness, and that I should not pull the wool over my eyes. The connection was broken before I managed to pull myself together. For a couple of minutes I stood there completely dazed with the telephone in my hand."

"Our man is going too far," I said reflectively. "One does not phone a lady at dawn. However, I must admit that I did feel lonely and sad."

She pressed my hand as if begging me to reassure her more effectively and I felt an urgent need to take her into my arms to protect her and to give her a greater share of the deep peace with which her presence filled me. "How he found out, the devil only knows," I added. "I hope at least that you don't suspect me again of being Joachim Stiller."

"Are you still angry about that?"

"It was not flattering, but I could understand it. We didn't know each other and I did my best not to attach any importance to your opinion of me."

"Do you think it important now?" she asked me point-blank, while extinguishing her cigarette. "It sounds rude, but I don't mean it like that..."

"I said that I did my best not to attach any importance to it," I replied. "But I admit frankly that the whole Stiller affair had got on my nerves, while it did in fact make me sad that someone like you was involved with those dull *Atomium* rascals..."

Spontaneously, I mean without calculation, I clasped her sweet face with both my hands. Later she told me that I looked sad although I was not aware of it myself. Her features seemed to become blurred through the intensity with which she looked at me with her astonishingly pure eyes. The sounds of the city which form the familiar background of my daily life seemed to have stopped a long while ago. Only her gray eyes were still there. Her gray shining eyes and the sound of her voice.

"I no longer have anything to do with them, Freek. Anything. I realized it only a short time ago. I could not go on living in that atmosphere of immaturity, pedantry, pseudo-artiness, and childish squabbles."

"No longer you say. But..."

"I broke my engagement not an hour ago. I have to get used to the thought gradually. Forgive me..." Her eyes overflowed with tears but it had nothing to do with the tearful scenes some women use to endear themselves to a man. "The end of an inexplicable mistake that lasted a year. I am a bit upset but there is nothing tragic about it. I just wanted to talk to someone I could trust..."

I knew that I had to remain silent, grateful for her trust in me, and full of the strange awareness, which slowly spread through my whole being, that I was much more deeply involved in this than she would dare let me know. I also knew that it could change suddenly into a poignant sensation of happiness such as I had never known before. Yet at the same time a melancholy feeling rose up in me, and seemed to delay this transformation. It was a feeling of melancholia that had a name...the name, really familiar to me for the first time in my life, of Joachim Stiller. I knew, although I was not at all afraid, that that name would never disappear completely from my life, just as the apostate probably suspects that God can never die out completely in his hormones. It really was a completely absurd awareness, difficult to reconcile with the certainty I felt at the same time that one gesture would be sufficient to call Simone Marijnissen mine and to forget everything else in her beautiful bare arms. To which must be added that I exercised exemplary self-control, that afternoon.

CHAPTER 11

Professor Schoenmakers

Geert Molijn's introduction worked miracles with Professor Schoen-makers. Just over an hour after I had phoned the Central Anti-quarian Research Laboratories in Brussels, I parked my car near the Jubelpark Museum and helped Simone get out. While my little Citroën sped along the freeway and I, true to my bad habit, raced all the huge pretentious American cars, we had not talked very much, but nevertheless I felt profoundly contented with her quiet presence, although I had hesitated to phone her first. I have often hesitated in my life, envious of people with uncomplicated, so-called straightforward natures who, regardless of obstacles, doggedly plod on to achieve their aims. But neither do I belong to that self-assured type of people who dispose of another's destiny in cold blood. I reminded myself that I had no claims to Simone, in spite of her broken engagement, even if she had come to me that afternoon of her own free will. I had never held to the view, as I reminded myself steadfastly, that even the most intimate relationship with a woman necessarily had to find its fulfillment in bed.

When we asked an attendant for directions it appeared that we were on the wrong side. Meanwhile it had begun to rain and the man advised us to walk through the Museum of Natural History. I have a soft spot for these nineteenth-century museums. They are among the few places where I become completely at ease—like a religious person in church, I imagine—more completely than in the open country where I always get the impression that I am only a casual passerby. We were the only visitors and if I had not had my appointment I would not have thought it a waste of time for us to spend the whole afternoon here, delighted like children over a stone lance head from the Neolithic Age, the bones of a late cave dweller with a hole in his skull, or the impressive horde of our primeval national ancestors, while the rain pattered soothingly on

77

the dome-shaped roof. However, we could not let Schoenmakers wait and I promised Simone, who was in a holiday mood and did not have the little worried furrow over her nose which had made me feel so unspeakably tender toward her from the beginning, that I would love to come back with her another time.

I had imagined Professor Schoenmakers, whose name I knew because of his radiographic and chemical work in the field of the history of art and archeology but especially because of his decisive report and testimony in a sensational trial about a faked Brueghel, to be slim, ascetic, and nearsighted. But he was in fact stocky and broad-shouldered like a wrestler—a friendly bear wearing socks—and his sparkling brown eyes, continually surrounded by little laughter wrinkles, made me feel that he could look straight through you, but without making you feel uncomfortable. He wore a pair of velvet trousers in which one could not detect a single pressed pleat and a loose tweed jacket that had known better days. Yet although he looked like a gentleman farmer who did not care about the way he dressed, I was aware that an aura of astonishing intellectual dynamism surrounded him. He received us in his enormous office where indescribable chaos prevailed: he had to move a few piles of books and papers before he could offer us a seat. The whole setting breathed peace and quiet which seemed to be a continuation of the unreal atmosphere in the museum. Although I had an ineradicable dislike of troubling a man like him with the trivialities that occupied my mind, I knew for certain that I could speak freely with him, as one can with a doctor who never forgets that the boundaries between body and soul are imaginary.

"It was Geert Molijn," I said, "who advised me to come to you, Professor. I want to ask you to do something for me, but I know it concerns a rather incredible story which you may possibly think completely childish. But quite frankly, not only my peace of mind depends on it but also that of Miss Marijnissen who has become inexplicably involved in this too."

The manner in which he looked at me was sufficient for me to realize that he was a very good man who intuitively sympathized with us.

"Please don't apologize, Mr. Groenevelt. I am pleased to become better acquainted with you. I don't have a lot of free time, but I count myself among your most loyal readers, I imagine. I know, moreover, that peace of mind is the most essential element in the life of a human being. The friends of my good Geert are also my friends."

"The beginning of our story is reminiscent of a not very convincing detective novel..."

"I am crazy about detective novels... Our work sometimes is a bit like a thriller, you know."

"One moment, Professor. I had thought of putting it in the hands of the police but on closer consideration it appeared to me that I did not have sufficient reason. Miss Marijnissen and I have recently been receiving letters at more or less regular intervals from someone who is unknown to us. Usually the contents are rather sibylline but very neatly composed and, when all is said and done, not really alarming at all. They are not threatening letters, as you will perhaps think—on the contrary, I would say..."

"Have you known each other long? Please forgive me if I am rude."

"Only a few weeks. One of the strange things about these peculiar messages is that the first one, received by Miss Marijnissen, already referred to me even though we had never met at that time. A few days ago, our man made use of the telephone for the first time..."

"Some persistent joker, then?"

"That seems to be the most likely explanation. I personally would therefore not attach great importance to them were it not that, however one looks at it, one is always left with one absolutely inexplicable element."

"You make me curious. I have always been an inquisitive fellow, you know."

"Inexplicable, unless it is part of an extremely sophisticated plan, the purpose of which is completely beyond my powers of imagination. I find it impossible to think that anyone, even an insane person, would spend so much energy on it. One of the letters addressed to me, you see, must have been, well..."

Suddenly it all seemed so absolutely absurd to me that I felt myself blushing with shame. Simone looked at me encouragingly, as if she was afraid that I would shrink back at the last moment, inhibited by the incredibility of what was to come. Our host too had noticed her glance.

"You need not be embarrassed, Mr. Groenevelt. I am most interested."

"Well, then, Professor... Everything seems to indicate that at least one of the letters of Joachim Stiller—for that is how this strange fellow signs himself—must have been written and posted about forty years ago. It sounds completely idiotic, I know..."

I was fidgeting restlessly on my chair and the palms of my hands were wet with perspiration. Schoenmakers continued to look at me full of interest. He gave no indication so far that he had any doubt about my mental capacities.

"What basis is there for your supposition?"

"At first I looked only at the stamp which was definitely current shortly after the First World War. These stamps, though they have been invalid for a very long time, have not completely disappeared and the Post Office cannot notice everything...But the affair really unnerved me when I noticed that the envelope had been stamped about forty years ago."

"One reads in the paper from time to time about articles which wander around the world in the mail for decades, in order to get from Brussels to Mechelen..."

"I have thought of that too, of course. But who could have known forty years ago, Professor, that an as yet unborn Freek Groenevelt would at one time live in Antwerp in the Koepoort Street? And who could allude to a newspaper article which appeared in *De Scheldebode* less than a week before the arrival of that curious letter?" I handed the intriguing document to the scholar and asked him to read the contents for himself. He fished out his glasses from the pocket of his jacket. While reading, he whistled in surprise like a mischievous boy. "Logically speaking, it cannot be anything else but a joke, Professor... And yet..."

He stared at me pensively and the expression in his eyes became remarkably gentle, as if he wanted to show in that way that my disquiet, my annoyance, or whatever I might call it, appeared completely understandable to him. "The letter *is* old," he said quietly but emphatically, "unless we have here an unbelievably clever forgery. I expect you want to find out exactly how old this letter may be?"

"That is in fact why we have come here so boldly, Professor. I did not know whom to turn to and Geert Molijn advised me..."

"Your patience will not be tried for very long. Will you excuse me for a moment? I will tell the people in the laboratory to start on this immediately. With the instruments we have, it is not difficult..."

He only stayed away for a few minutes but meanwhile we sat staring speechlessly in front of us, besieged by the most contrary feelings. On the one hand we hoped that the examination would prove that we had been worrying without real cause, but on the other hand the thought bewildered us that the possibility of the absurd would be established with scientific precision. We were relieved when Schoenmakers joined us again.

"In half an hour we will know for certain," he said cheerfully. "What we can do with papyrus of four thousand years ago without great difficulty is not even a routine job where a letter from Mr. Stiller is concerned..."

"I don't like it," Simone said, "I have never liked it. What does this certainty you are talking about mean? How are we to go on living if it is proved that you are right?"

"But the Professor also alluded to forgery," I suggested. "What else could it be but a forgery? We have come here, like a hypochondriac to his physician. Deep inside he knows very well that he is worrying about the figments of his imagination. He consults the physician in order to be freed from his fancies. Is that not so, Professor?"

"Whatever the explanation, we have to wait for the result of the test. It won't be very long..."

"Do you really think it is possible, then, that...," Simone asked, almost stammering; I could see her hands trembling as she fumbled with the fastening of her handbag.

"I am very sorry not to be able to reassure a charming young lady like you immediately," the scholar answered in a paternal tone of voice. "But even at its worst—I mean, if my suspicion turns out to be true—that letter need not frighten you. I am not an expert in these matters, but I imagine that the parapsychologists have by now collected so much factual evidence that even the intellectually mature cannot disregard the possibility that forty years ago a certain Mr. Stiller possessed a pronounced talent for looking into the future. I am sure Geert Molijn can tell you more about this..."

"Miss Marijnissen is a Doctor in Mathematics," I said, smiling with an effort. "She prefers the exact sciences."

"The fantastic does not intimidate me," Simone interrupted. "Modern mathematics too is fantastic, if you like. I could conceive of a Stiller with the gift of seeing into the future...But I feel alarmed by the crazy, yet somewhat logical, coherence of this whole story. After all, each letter is a message with reference to the future..."

"Stiller's letter: a message in a bottle on the waves of time...?" Schoenmakers suggested dreamily.

"If you like...But one does not telephone out of the past!"

"Joachim Stiller need not necessarily be dead," I suggested without much conviction. "He may very well still be among us. Perhaps we have already passed him several times in the street. Unless, being a gentle maniac, he is locked up safely somewhere in a mental home."

"Since we are giving free rein to our imagination anyway," our host suggested whimsically, "we merely have to find a solution for the delivery by mail, about forty years late, it's true, but nonetheless very much at the right moment, if I have not misunderstood Mr. Groenevelt. Perhaps Miss Marijnissen can help me here—I am thinking of the calculus of probabilities and suchlike..."

"It is impossible," replied Simone, who did not wish to consider Schoenmaker's contemplation as a little joke. "It is completely impossible. It is a thousand times more likely that a most elaborate trick is being played on us..."

At that moment the door was opened by one of the Professor's assistants. He was a handsome sporty young man whom we liked immediately because of his unpretentiousness.

"I'm sorry for the delay, Professor," he said. "Taking into account the possibility of an insignificant divergence, as you know, this document must be thirty-eight years old. To make certain, we have checked three times, not only the ink and the paper of the envelope, but also that of the text itself."

I shuddered. I saw Simone grow pale, although she controlled herself.

"One moment," Schoenmakers interrupted his assistant. "Let me introduce you to Miss Marijnissen and Mr. Groenevelt, yes, Freek Groenevelt, the writer...This is Doctor Walter Coppieters, my chief assistant and, if no obscure political forces come along to spoil things, my successor, when I shall be devoting all my time, like the old Belgians, to fishing and beekeeping...Listen a moment, old boy...yes, do sit down...just throw that mess on the floor...You will have noticed of course that it is a rather peculiar letter. Has Sipido taken a look at it?"

"Christiaan Sipido?" I asked in amazement, "the graphologist for the Attorney General's office?..."

"Yes...he is primarily a paleographer and therefore belongs to our staff. He only works incidentally for the Court of Justice. Has he been able to leave his hobbyhorse in its stable?"

"Quite frankly, no, Professor. But if you had not given any instructions in that direction, I would have thought that he had exceeded his authority."

"No formality, Coppieters...Our guests must be thinking that I am a cannibal..."

The young man winked at me which gave his handsome face a most endearing expression and confirmed my feeling that the scholar could no doubt flare up from time to time with considerable violence, but nonetheless in a fatherly way. Coppieters picked up the intercom telephone, dialed a number, and asked his colleague to come to the boss's office. The familiar "boss" sounded so friendly that I could well understand Schoenmakers not making any objection to it, even in the presence of a third party. Sipido was a rather inconspicuous but dapper little fellow. He reminded me of a verger or an undertaker, but behind his heavy glasses his eyes sparkled with sheer intelligence and joy of living. After introducing us and describing the situation in outline, Schoenmakers asked him what he thought of Stiller's handwriting.

"Do you think it could be the writing of a mentally disturbed person?" I asked when I noticed that he shrugged his shoulders a little impatiently as if he did not know precisely where to begin. "For the most obvious solution must be that this letter was written by a maniac. But on the other hand the writing is so balanced that I am wondering if..."

"The beauty and harmony of it are not decisive, you know, Mr. Groenevelt. I have often seen specimens of the handwriting of the insane and the criminal which could very well have come from a schoolteacher of the last century."

"Is that of interest to us in this particular case?" asked the scholar.

"Yes and no, Professor. It is true that the handwriting of Mr.

Groenevelt's letter is of a scholastic perfection, but this in itself would not be very significant, were it not for..."

"Well?"

"Sometimes I get lost too, you see...I have the impression that this Stiller is a case completely on its own. If it is really important to Mr. Groenevelt, I would be willing to send him within twenty-four hours an analysis and explanation that is as extensive as possible..."

"A few general remarks now would be most helpful," I replied. "We don't want to cause you too much trouble. But a friend of mine, an amateur graphologist, thought that Stiller's handwriting gives evidence of a complete lack of personality. Or is that nonsense?"

"That is not completely true to the facts but such a mistake is understandable. I would even say that your friend is a good judge of such matters. And yet I can tell you with comparative certainty that, on the contrary, your man possesses not only an astonishingly strong, but also a disconcertingly balanced, personality—so balanced that it makes my head reel, if you want my opinion. He is completely the opposite of the abnormal man you apparently take him for. Never before have I seen a handwriting that demonstrates such absolute moral and spiritual unity. I am quite at sea. My conclusion has nothing to do with the calligraphic perfection of the letter. The author might have written in terrible scrawls, but in deepest essence they would show the same characteristics..."

"Send Mr. Groenevelt the detailed analysis in any case," Schoenmakers concluded. "And let me have a look at it first. I find it an intriguing story, you know."

Silently we walked along the broad gravel path to the car. The sun had broken through the clouds and the fantastic nineteenth-century architecture of the museum buildings with the pompous triumphal arch in the middle outlined against the limitless sky showed unreal contrasts of light and shadow. We both seemed to have the feeling that we were the last inhabitants of a disrupted world where time had stopped. We walked hand in hand, like children frightened in the dark.

CHAPTER 12

The Concert

Never shall I convince myself that what happened afterwards between Simone and me can be considered separately from Joachim
Stiller's appearance in our lives. When I was younger, love and
passion played a moderately important part in everything I wrote.
Looking back, I realize that I was giving expression to my dream
fantasies. I also know now that my diffidence toward the real world
was not altogether unrelated to the fact that I experienced in my
stories the things that were mostly kept from me by the reality of
everyday life. Nonetheless, there are some critics, able to see beyond
the end of their noses, who have from time to time drawn attention
to the fact that as a young man a constant need of purity remained
alive in me—not the purity of impotence or barren denial but
arising from an intuitive conviction, beyond the need of proof,
that there must exist the possibility of an exceptional perfection
in love, capable of withstanding familiarity and wear and tear,
and immune to the corrosive influence of daily contact. In the
course of time my skepticism gained ground in that field too. But
that evening, while we lay listening to the carillon of the nearby
cathedral above the city—the carillon that sounded every quarter
of an hour, delicate in the night air like a filigree of sound in the
square of the open window—the dream of my adolescence and the
first years of my manhood rose up again in me, and with it the sad
awareness that with Simone I was being given a last but definite
chance to conquer an apparently long-forfeited Ultima Thule, not
forfeited because of unworthiness, but because life puts up a blank
wall between reality and the dream of the child we once were and
which survives in some of us. I still did not want to acknowledge
the reality of Stiller's existence which had been thrust across my
quiet life like a strange latticework. I still refused to accept as
self-evident his intervention in my relationship with the beautiful

young woman, whose body was languidly stretched out against
mine. But, although it did not disturb me for the present, I knew
nonetheless that he had something to do with it—even if he was
only a shadow created by our imagination. It probably sounds
strange, but when I recall that first night and Simone's serene
expression, her head resting in the hollow of my arm and my face
bent over it (full of attention, and guidance too, for the ancient
mystery in which we had participated with so astonishing a com-
pleteness that afterwards we had stroked each others' features
rapturously and full of surprise, as if to make sure that it was not
a dream that had led us astray), the thought springs to mind again
and again that my life up till then had merely been one inevitable
growth toward the perfection of this hour.

Contrary to habit I had driven very slowly on the way back. I
wanted to make the time we had together last as long as possible,
although I could not find words to dispel the feeling of bewilderment that had been with us since we left Schoenmakers. The deep
dejection I felt paralyzed my good intentions of reassuring her. That
is how it was till we got to Boom, where we were kept waiting in
front of a drawbridge. We had already been waiting quite a while
but I kept the engine running. Then it came to pass that she
turned the ignition off and put her arms around my neck. I knew
that she was not one of those enterprising women, that it could
surely not be her intention to present me with a fait accompli,
but that she looked for safety with me, that she wanted to make sure
of my presence and take care that this time we would not part
with so much left unsaid between us. Only when the cars behind
mine began to blow their horns in annoyance did we realize that
the lights at the bridge were green again. She put her head on my
shoulder and I noticed in the mirror, which I gave a little push,
how she kept her eyes tightly shut, as if she wanted to concentrate
on a completely new and powerful realization still belonging to
silence and frail in its novel appearance. The moment had come to
break our silence.

"Joachim Stiller be hanged," I said full of bravado. "It depends
only on us whether he exists or no. To hell with the man. It's
about time we stopped worrying about such nonsense. I've got a
brilliant idea. We'll quickly pack our bags and be off to Paris this
very evening. Around daybreak we'll be having breakfast together

with the market vendors in a small restaurant near Les Halles
which stays open all night. Or would you think it indecent to
come with me?"

"To the end of the world if you want me to," she replied, reck-
lessly but full of determination. "But in this case it would look too
much like an escape, Freek. I am prepared to come with you, wherever you want to go. But let's not take to flight because of that man,
even if we convince ourselves that it has nothing to do with him..."

"You're right," I answered. "We would have a wonderful time
together. But under no circumstances shall we take to our heels.
Why should we? The summer isn't over yet. Anyway, I'm not leaving you alone tonight. I'm counting on it that we are going to
eat together in town. Agreed?"

We went by way of her house because she wanted to put on a
different dress. She left the door of her bedroom open while she
changed and I waited for her. It was a special evening for both of
us and I was aware that she responded instinctively to the precepts
of a moving esthetic ritual that must not be interfered with. But
I felt how my hands were trembling as I lit a cigarette. She looked
beautiful and thanks to her inborn dignity it did not seem at all
wrong that she had bound her hair in a single long braid reaching
down to her waist; it gave her an air which was girlish and extremely
sophisticated all at once.

In the smart restaurant "De blauwe Schuyte" in the Keizer
Street, where the beams of the ceiling and the candlelight seem
less artificial than in other similar places, I took pleasure in the
fact that at this rather late hour we were not the only guests and
that Simone was regarded with interest. I noticed a few people
who were vaguely familiar to me and to whom I had never spoken
before, but now they seemed to be making a point of greeting me
emphatically and even rather intimately as if we were in the habit
of always slapping each other on the shoulder in friendly fashion.
Thanks to my companion, literature and journalism seemed to have
gained considerably in prestige. I was boyishly proud of her, even
though I had asserted in earlier days that only little old gentlemen,
playing their last trump, like to create a stir by being seen in a
restaurant with a beautiful woman—at least, if they can still manage
that. Although, as I told her, the idea of getting older had often
obsessed me after my thirty-fifth birthday, I could feel very strongly

that evening that I was still young and had not yet drained the cup of life's experience, whether it tasted bitter or sweet.

"Wherever did you get the idea that you were old?" Simone interrupted me with a laugh. "Did you know, Freek, that you still have the eyes of a child when you look at me like that?"

"I haven't got the faintest notion of how my eyes look at the moment," I answered. "But I drink to yours, Simone. I drink to the gray clarity of your eyes, which not only make me fall in love but which also move me very deeply, because they remind me of my mother..."

She put her cool hand on mine. She did not need words to make me understand that she realized very well how inside my horizon a place had remained free for a woman like her, a woman whom I had waited for and who would not make dim the picture of my first love. The gesture with which she put her hand on the back of mine, without presumption, but tender and reassuring, was a decisive factor in our life. No lie stood between us, there were no quicksands of self-deception or recklessness. Even without words we knew that our fate was sealed. After coffee we walked through the city again, hand in hand like children; it was so natural that passersby did not even seem to notice it—as far as I saw any passersby.

It was a bright blue, quite warm evening after a day of pale sunshine. We sat for a while in a small artistic bar with a lot of oak wood and leaded windows on the tiny Saint Niklaas Square; afterwards she took it for granted that she would accompany me to my room. Quietly she undressed. Despite my desire for her, my emotions were so absolutely poised and balanced that I still found time to laugh about her funny but provocatively small nylon panties. While we lay beside each other and I stroked her with fingers that with their nerve ends hardly touched her well-developed, fresh body, I asked her why she suddenly looked at me so sadly. She put her arm around my neck and replied, her face pressed against mine, that she was terribly sorry, that... her voice broke. "What is past is not of the slightest importance," I said consolingly, "unless you yourself still attach importance to the memory. As far as I am concerned, I don't harbor any primitive prejudices. It is not possible to live without the lesson of disillusionment. At this moment we only live for the present. Apart from one thing, Simone.

It is not too late yet to think of the consequences, the possible consequences..."

Abruptly she looked at me. It made me happy that she smiled again. "I have thought of the consequences, you know...In novels and films it is hardly ever mentioned. Strange really, for it's something so essential...Of course I've thought about it. I have even involuntarily calculated the chances—a tendency stronger than my will. Probably a distortion caused by a profession in mathematics. But you see"—she slowly traced the outline of my lips with her index finger—"I *have* thought of it, but I'm not afraid of it... Surely, you don't want me to put my clothes back on again, do you?"

She had not put her clothes back on again that night and I still sat bent over her, as if I had never known before what it meant to possess a woman to the depths of her body and soul, without it seeming necessary even to make a distinction between the two. She had dozed off, her mouth slightly open, so that I could partly see her regular pearly white teeth; she was breathing quietly, the fingers of her right hand spread out over her breast as if searching for the beat of her heart, which was quiet again now. When the carillon in the tower began again, she opened her eyes without surprise and pulled me against her.

"The carillon," she whispered, "do you hear how pure it sounds? You'd swear that the sound was much stronger than before..."

"Perhaps the wind has turned," I answered. "Or no, we were not interested in it before..."

We embraced each other again with vehement urgency, but we did not immediately become so absorbed in each other that we did not notice how this time the carillon knew no end to its play. Involuntarily I sat up again.

"That's not the tower chimes," I said, perplexed, "all the bells of the carillon are playing. It's incredible at this hour of the night." I looked at my watch. "Twenty past one. I can't understand it; it's never happened before."

Driven by curiosity I went and stood by the window and Simone timidly joined me. Protectively I put my arm around her shoulders. When she shivered I gave her a pair of my pyjamas and put on a dressing gown myself. Tucking up the sleeves that were far too long for her, she asked whether I was thinking too that something was wrong with the mechanism in the tower.

"That's out of the question," I replied. "The small carillon which chimes every quarter of an hour is mechanical, but only a carillon-neur can play the big carillon. Anyway, you are right. The sound is unusually strong. I expect the whole neighborhood is awake by now."

Strangely enough, no one appeared to be surprised or worried by the unusual concert. Down in the street, the late passersby quietly went on their way, as if deaf. Not a light was switched on any-where, no one appeared in the open windows and the others re-mained indifferently closed.

We saw the cathedral tower rise up before us, sky-high and gleaming like silver. The clarity of the theatrical full moon seemed to cover the landscape of roofs with a thin snowdrift, and I had the feeling that there was an inexplicable link between this strange, unreal blue light and the growing and diminishing sounds, appar-ently born out of nothing a hundred meters above the nocturnal city. I have often heard the carillon here on summer evenings, sometimes against my will, for only a tiny fraction of my far from underdeveloped musical sense is satisfied by this national brand of sound production; at best I listen to it as one listens to the wind or to the breakers beating against a palisade. But this time it was truly music in the absolute sense of the word, almost organ music, broadly spiraling down and spreading itself in waxing and slowly waning spheres over the apparently quite deserted city. I had not seen any passersby for a long time and there were no lighted windows anywhere. We heard tens, perhaps hundreds of greater and smaller bells enlarge upon the original melody, but I could not place it, although it had something vaguely familiar to me, like a name which perversely hesitates on the tip of the tongue or on the edge of one's memory. We stood listening so intently that I com-pletely lost all sense of time. I wondered if we had stood, fascinated, by the window for an hour already or if only a few minutes had gone by since Simone had opened her eyes in surprise. I looked at my watch. It was still twenty past one. In surprise I put it to my ear and found that it had stopped; but the gesture made it start ticking again. At the same time the carillon music died out, unnaturally soft, I thought to myself, in about the same way as a melody is faded out on the radio. I shivered inside from a vague mixture of joy and sadness, connected with my remotest memories.

For a moment I was again the child of long ago, holding my father's hand and standing, together in the Sunday afternoon rain among many other men in overcoats, on a railway viaduct, and before us, visible between a few houses, the flat surface of the training field outside the city walls of that time; above it was the gray outline of dozens of balloons, shackled like dead, monstrously swollen fish to the bottom of an underwater valley. Later I realized that it must have been the start of the Gordon-Bennett race or something like that. There was a wintry atmosphere, although it must have been summer of course, but above all there was my childlike amazement at the number of people my father knew who came to have a chat with him—neighbors, I expect, from our small rural suburb where he had always lived and where I myself grew up.

Then it was suddenly half past one and quietly the old familiar carillon rang out again, real this time.

"You'll catch cold," I said, "let's go inside again."

I drew the curtains and switched on the lamp above my writing desk. When she nestled her head again on my shoulder I noticed that her face was wet with tears. Although I did not know the cause of her sorrow, it made me feel more intimately attached to her than ever before. I said quietly, as if to myself, in order that it would not sound presumptuous or sentimental: "I am not a man of adventures, Simone. I have always been a lone wolf and one can be mistaken in loneliness too. Tonight, neither of us has made a mistake."

"I don't doubt myself, otherwise what happened tonight between us would never have occurred...But I'm afraid—no, not afraid of the consequences, not afraid that I have been mistaken in you; you must believe that of me, Freek..."

"Of what or of whom are you afraid?" I asked despondently.

She slowly raised her eyes to mine from under her velvety lashes, as if filled with repressed panic.

"I am afraid of that carillon music, afraid that we alone heard it. I am afraid of Joachim Stiller. His shadow lies over everything that happens between us, even the dearest moments that do not permit a witness. I cannot endure that thought..."

I was not given time to think of a reassuring answer. The telephone rang shrilly through the silence. I told myself that it must be a mistake and said in a level tone of voice, though my heart was pounding, "Hello, Groenevelt speaking."

I could have sworn that I had heard that voice before but not for all the riches in the world could I have said where or when. It seemed centuries ago. Holding my breath with tension, I heard the voice say, "My name must not be a trial to you. Come what may, one day I shall free you from all fear. Equanimity does not depend entirely on me. You must find it in yourselves. Preserve your confidence. Dare to win. Nothing is as yet irrevocable..."

"Hello," I raged, hoarse with nervousness, "hello, who's that speaking? This joke has gone on long enough, damn it. I'll call the police..."

But I was storming against a dead mouthpiece.

Despondently I put down the receiver.

"Was it...?" Simone asked with suddenly feverish eyes.

"Some joker," I replied gloomily and shrugged my shoulders insincerely. "Perhaps a colleague of mine, you never know, who saw us go into the house together. You could call it an expression of bad taste..."

She did not believe me, of course. In silence we waited for dawn.

CHAPTER 13

The Cocktail Party

Early in the morning we fell asleep and woke up when the sun stood high above the city. Although we made love once again that morning, it was mainly to dispel our fear. The radiant summer's day made everything different again and when I opened the curtains, in order to allow Simone to be woken up by the sun, I knew that life was still worth living and that I could face it again. Intently, I watched her as she woke up and when I took her in my arms it was clear that for her too the strange events of the previous night had been reduced to the proportions of an incident about which we would laugh together tomorrow and which had not damaged the wonderful certainty of our love. Even under the shower we were still playing around and if she had not pushed me out of the kitchen we probably would not have had much of a breakfast.

We agreed that I would make it as brief as possible at the paper and that in the meantime she would collect some indispensable toilet articles. We would have to see what would happen then, but it was an established fact for both of us that a separation lasting longer than a few hours was absolutely unbearable and to be rejected without further consideration.

In the pressroom I collected the most topical articles from my stock of copy that had already been set up and I decided that I had done enough for about three days.

There was a telephone call for me just as I was about to slip diplomatically away. It was with relief that I recognized Wiebrand Zijlstra's voice.

"You must forgive me, Freek, for not contacting you since we last met," he said. "I have been terribly busy. Do you remember that little man on the Oude Vaar Square?..." I vaguely mumbled something in agreement. "Well, I was quite right, you know. Everything has gone smoothly... I'm holding a kind of semiofficial press conference this afternoon. No, I don't want it written about yet...

It's more like an introduction. Anyway, apart from journalists there are going to be a lot of art lovers and connoisseurs present. I'm counting on your being there!"

Annoyed, I said that his invitation had come rather late and that I already had an appointment, but we were soon agreed that Simone would come with me. She did not make any objections, because she understood very well that life went on and that I could not pull out of all my commitments; she was really quite pleased to accompany me and to appear for the first time in society more or less officially and without shame as my lover—that is how she put it, with satisfaction. She took a wonderful afternoon dress out of her suitcase, so crammed that its weight had obliged her to take a taxi. I took care not to spoil her pleasure, perhaps without justification, by telling her right away that Zijlstra, incalculable as ever, yet at the same time full of calculation, would receive his guests in a dilapidated gin distillery—long since, as far as I knew, half in ruins—which stood in the neighborhood of the old southern docks.

It was a miserable alley with the dreary brick walls of warehouses and industrial plants on both sides, where poor children stood gaping open-mouthed at the gleaming cars. My ex-schoolfriend welcomed us with decorative emphasis and ceremoniously kissed Simone's hand, but when he stealthily winked at me afterwards, as if he knew precisely what was going on, I could have boxed his ears with pleasure, even though I could not help admiring the way in which he had left nothing to chance. My colleagues made no secret of their skepticism and wondered out loud what that damned Zijlstra might be up to. But the numerous fine ladies, accompanied by serious or sheepish-looking elderly gentlemen who seemed to be rather self-conscious, cooed with pure enthusiasm as they waded carefully through the mud of the neglected courtyard, partly overgrown with thistles, dead nettles, wild sorrel, and other thriving weeds. I felt oppressed by a humiliating awareness of vague complicity, but kept quiet for the time being, for Simone appeared to be rather enjoying the whole situation.

With too many airs and graces for my liking, Wiebrand led us to a building of weather-beaten brickwork, transformed into an impressive studio which was more than large enough to house a master of the Renaissance with all his pupils. I recognized the shabby little man immediately. Somewhat dazed, he stood in a corner, dressed in an overall which in my opinion had been deliberately covered with paint, as if he had stopped work for a moment by pure chance, and stared numbly from behind his glasses at the elegant visitors who for the present did not show the least interest in him or the pictures that had been hung up on the wall. Zijlstra had not been completely wrong. In scarcely a couple of weeks he had apparently taught his protégé, with the help of a few kitchen recipes—I suddenly remembered now that he himself had been at the art academy for a while—to paint an apparently virtuoso background on a canvas and how to add to this a plastic effect by mixing pebbles, ash, river sand, and possibly other kinds of muck in with the paint. On this extraordinary foundation, which was nonetheless well suited for the purpose since it had the look of a dirty, worn-out wall, the little graffito man had had his fling, evidently without repudiating his primitive sources of inspiration. In this way the walls of the studio gave a sample, as enormous as it was grotesque, of the most astonishing urinal eroticism, scratched spasmodically into the paint with a nail, or so it seemed. They were mostly human figures with exaggeratedly large or small heads. All these ghostly or demonic hydro- and microcephalics of the male and female sex, materialized from the dreams of a man obsessed, exhibited such pronounced sexual features that I felt embarrassed for Simone, not so much because I regarded her as a prude, but because all this gave me the impression of a horrible mental deviation and made a mockery of all artistic decency; I had to admit, however, that the newly made artist had given form in a consistent way to the things that wriggled and fermented under his bird-like skull, like maggots and fungi in a dung heap.

"We shall have to summon all our sense of humor, if we don't want to run away," I said. "If it becomes too weird for you we'll let Mr. Wiebrand go to hell and we'll get out immediately."

"Don't worry," Simone said, "all this doesn't make the slightest impression on me. It doesn't impress me, but I feel sorry for the wretch who created them. Do you think he really lives continually in some infernal limbo? Anyway, the boys of *Atomium* would think all this was wonderful . . ."

"Wonderful, really wonderful, don't you think?" Zijlstra shouted gleefully, and I suspected him of having listened in on our conversation. "We'll be the talk of the town before the next few weeks are over... Once we've got that far, criticism and discussion will follow automatically. The main thing is to get a few bureaucrats from Brussels interested with a view to official exhibitions abroad... I've discovered a gold mine, almost without working expenses!"

I looked into the whites of Wiebrand's eyes and said, without raising my voice, "What you are doing is revolting, even if it brings you a fortune. It is horrible to abuse a poor wretch like this, even if he is another Van Gogh. I'm not thinking of the stupid idiots you are fooling. They don't deserve any better. But I'm thinking of that retarded scrawler, of that piece of human misery who's being exhibited like a calf with two heads at a fun fair..."

The little man had come closer with dragging feet, shy and not quite grasping the situation, but from his attitude I concluded that his employer had beforehand impressed on his inaccessible mind how he was to behave. I noticed how Simone shrank back inuitively and how she involuntarily felt for my hand. "Come, my dear Groenevelt," Wiebrand protested, aggrieved. "You are grossly exaggerating. On the contrary, I am Siegfried's guardian angel— imagine, he's called Siegfried, that's what comes of that local Wagner cult of ours, believe it or not. I can show you, black on white, isn't it, Siegfried?... No, old boy, don't try to answer... He is deaf and dumb, and also a complete imbecile, as you may have noticed; he's also got a touch of epilepsy. But Siegfried is a good fellow, although I have to watch him when there are women around. When there are women near, he goes raving mad sometimes. I thought at first that a model would inspire him, but it inspired him in the wrong way. The girl fled into the courtyard with nothing on, and I had to lock him up in the studio. It was very spectacular, but it happened six months too soon..."

I did not want to make a quarrel and gritted my teeth, but Simone felt intuitively that I was sick with revulsion. She stroked my hand soothingly. Wiebrand judged that it was time to create a diversion. He steered us to the buffet "to drink to the health of the master," as he put it, with obvious irony. I drained my cocktail at one draft to hide my revulsion and pity. It was a pity, violent and absolute, which reminded me of my schooldays when, instinctively, I had also taken the side of the weaklings, the hungry ones with dirty necks and filthy noses, whenever I noticed again and again with bewilderment how teachers regularly used them as scapegoats; later, at high school, I became fiercely indignant when teachers used the clumsy and slow ones as an outlet for their astonishingly obtuse humor, afflicted as they were with a craving for power unworthy of people who pride themselves on belonging to the intellectual class. Yet many people mistake my revolt, almost completely ineffectual in such circumstances, for an irritating arrogance. In the course of time I have resigned myself to this situation and perhaps it is best so, with my apparent pride as an indispensable armor covering my vulnerability in what is, after all, a rather crappy world.

When Wiebrand Zijlstra undertakes to do something, he does it thoroughly. As the gathering increasingly took on the character of an animated party and the first signs of drunkenness began to show, becoming apparent, among other things, through the re-shuffling of many couples, he went from group to group, not just to do his duty as a host in the proper way, but also to point out to those present, in confidence and probably with the utmost secrecy, the very special nature of his discovery. He beamed with satisfaction and elicited little shrieks of amazement, disbelief, and simulated horror from the ladies, who were gradually getting redder and redder, by whispering something into their ear from time to time. Simone asked me if he really was a friend of mine. She seemed relieved when I pointed out to her the casual and sporadic nature of our relationship.

"Forgive me, Freek," she said, "I didn't want to meddle in your affairs, but that man is not well-disposed toward people..."

The moment had come for Zijlstra to produce the champagne, and he listened with delight to the popping of the corks, as if it was the fusillade with which he was to surmount the barricades on the road to fortune. When the last crack sounded I was struck by the surprised expression on the face of the majordomo (or whatever these fellows are called) who stood staring in bewilderment at an empty bottle in his hand.

And almost at the same time I noticed how the picture dealer clutched his arm with a baffled expression on his face, which immediately afterwards became twisted with pain, while a quickly spreading bloodstain became visible in the pearl-gray material of his sleeve. It was a moment before the cheerful tittle-tattle of the conversation died out. On the staircase which led to the floor above or to an attic stood the little graffito man like an animal driven into a corner, even grayer and more insignificant than before, shyly holding a large army revolver in his hand. In the void created by the silence a woman began to scream. Everything now happened with dizzying speed. Ignoring the danger, Wiebrand Zijlstra raced up the stairs leaving a bright trail of blood on the ocher-colored floor. There was a brief but violent bumping noise in the attic above our heads, as though a struggle was taking place there. And as we all stood listening together, sober and as if petrified, desperate and bewildered, there were two more shots, one shortly after the other. I am not a hero by any means, as may be abundantly clear from this tale, but nonetheless I was the only one who was willing to dash to my schoolfriend's aid, even though Simone stubbornly held on to my arm. She only let go when our host unexpectedly came down the stairs again, deathly pale, but smiling and stiffly upright as if he wished to keep up appearances even in these circumstances. "On the roof," he said, and his voice hardly trembled, "escaped and climbed out of the attic window onto the roof. I've taken the revolver."

Despite the fact that he was staggering and I feared the worst, he was the first to go outside. People wanted to restrain him, but he said there would be plenty of time later on. We followed him to the courtyard where we saw with horror how the little man, defying all laws of equilibrium, was climbing up in an attempt to reach the ridge of the high and steep tiled roof; he was driven by an incomprehensible hope, for nowhere was the distance to nearby buildings short enough to offer him even an imaginary chance of escape.

"Phone the fire station," I heard a man say, "the fire station and the police. Where is the nearest telephone? . . ." It was already too late. As he stretched out his arms to a chimney shaft, he underestimated the distance. Grotesquely he grasped at the air, tottered like a drunkard—it lasted improbably long—after which with an inhuman cry he tumbled down along the tiles and crashed to his death with a dull but horrifyingly audible thud on the cement loading platform in front of the building. Wiebrand and I were the only ones who found the courage necessary to run to him.

"The idiot has broken his neck," Wiebrand shouted, but I did not answer and tried to lift up the upper part of the little man's body.

It was only a question of human respect. I did not doubt that he had died instantly. But although he was bleeding profusely from his mouth and nose, and his miserable skull seemed to me one horrible mass of pulp, he opened his eyes behind the cheap crooked glasses which miraculously had not been damaged. At first the dying man stared at Zijlstra in confusion, as if from a land too far for us to reach. But then recognition followed slowly and his colorless glance was gradually filled with such abysmal hatred that I felt myself to be the indiscreet witness to a drama which could not be put into words. At that moment a factory siren nearby began to wail heartrendingly. It was then, that the dying man looked at me. He tried to stammer something, it seemed to me, but it was obvious that it was the death rattle of a deaf-mute. Disconcerted, I realized that he seemed to be making an effort to smile at me, a faint but unmistakable smile, as if I was a good friend of his, had been for years, and as if he wanted to show his gratitude to me because I did not let him die alone, like a dog, I thought. I am certain that I did not hear wrongly. With an effort, but articulating quite distinctly, he stammered: "Stiller... Tell Sti..."

Then his eyes broke and glazed over fixedly and he died with a violent convulsion, like a fish outside its element.

"He said something, damn it," Zijlstra said. "The siren made too much noise. It hurt him. 'Stiller,' he said, 'Stiller.' Would you believe it!"

"I didn't hear it," I muttered noncommittally, and took off the little glasses to close the jelly-like eyes.

CHAPTER 14

The Hypothesis Builders

I had done my best to make the story sound as simple as possible. Simone too had shown exemplary restraint. Her discreet interruptions, which confined themselves to the heart of the matter, sometimes shed an unexpected light on my summary of what had happened. Despite my confusion, the thought had passed through my mind that this might well be her usual way of speaking in the classroom when posing and analyzing a mathematical problem, and this amused me and endeared her to me. In the meantime I knew that fear had permanently taken root in our inner being, although neither of us alluded to it directly. I asked myself defiantly if there always had to be something standing in the way of the perfect union of two people, in mind as well as in body—and if happiness was in fact an illusion, as hypochondriacal moralists maintain.

"Yes, it is an extraordinary story," Molijn muttered partly to himself, polishing three gin glasses with a towel and holding them up one by one to the light, his eyes screwed up.

"Up till now I have never doubted that it must have been a joke, backed in the most unlikely manner by a strange coincidence," I said. "Even Professor Schoenmakers and his staff can make mistakes. At a pinch, I would even let myself be convinced, Geert, that I was a victim of an hallucination when I heard that little man utter Stiller's name. But as far as the carillon is concerned, surely we can't both have been subject to the same delusion?"

"I don't know... There are reports of similar phenomena which have been observed by a whole mass of people."

"Freek is forgetting one detail," Simone interrupted quietly. "Before we came here, he asked the chaplain of the cathedral why the big carillon was playing last night."

"The good man looked terribly surprised and seemed to think I was not quite right in the head. He assured me that there was no question of the big carillon having been played last night. But anyway, that rather confirms the hallucination theory. You see, Geert, Simone and I, we are both healthy and even stable people. We are not neurotic, damn it."

Simone gently pressed my hand and it moved me that she added, without false shame, what I had left out for her sake: "I know you are Freek's best friend, Mr. Molijn. That is why I hope you won't think it improper of me, but last night was a special night for us..."

"Your trust makes an old man like me happier than he can tell you, Simone," Geert answered, "and I suggest that we stop once and for all with this 'Mr.' and 'Miss.' Believe me, your happiness lies close to my heart. But to come to the point. Simone wants to make me realize, I suspect, how..."

· "How at that moment we had no thought left for Stiller, how we were full of each other only," I completed his train of thought, "and less than ever susceptible to visions and delusions. I think I'd rather it were a maniac, some madman who pursued us and, if need be, would have come to some arrangement with the carillonneur."

It was absurd. Listening to my own words I could hear immediately that it was absurd.

"I would give anything to be able to reassure you," the book dealer said, "believe me, anything. But a joke...? No, I can't see how it could be a joke. But one never knows... Perhaps it would be a good idea to make a detailed chronological table of the successive events, but I don't really think that that would get us much further."

I hesitated a while before I said what had been on my mind for some time. I knew that in a sense it would be a capitulation and I was afraid of a defeat that would bring us to the border areas of a land of obscurity and madness.

"Listen," I said, and I got the impression that I was stammering, "listen, Geert. I don't like to ask you this. My nerves must be in a pretty bad state, otherwise I wouldn't mention it. Do you think we must look for an explanation in...well, in the supernatural?"

Molijn stared into space for a while and was silent, but I could see from the emphasis with which he took the cork out of the flask and filled the glasses that he regarded my question as an obvious one, but that he understood at the same time how difficult it was for me to conquer a feeling of inborn repulsion and of humiliation.

"I drink to your happiness," he said. "You are going through a difficult time, but I drink nonetheless to your happiness. For you have been born to be happy together. Oh, Freek, the supernatural? Where does the supernatural begin for you, where for Simone, and where for me?"

"Professor Schoenmakers suggested something about a parapsychological explanation. I didn't want to go into it then. I was surprised that a man like he could get such an idea. Up till then I had regarded parapsychology as a subject one reads about in books, maybe without disapproval, but at the same time without believing in it oneself—books which discuss phenomena never personally observed by the author..."

"I wish I could reassure you with a much more obvious explanation," Molijn replied.

"I've got into the state of mind now," I muttered despondently, "where I could even accept a parapsychological explanation. You know about these things, don't you?"

"I've more or less kept up with the literature. But to be quite frank, I cannot immediately think of a phenomenon, recognized by specialists as at least worth mentioning, with which I can compare the case of Stiller. Yet you yourself alluded a while ago to an almost incredible coincidence..."

"I vaguely remember something from my course in psychology for the prelims," Simone suggested hesitatingly. "Jung, if I'm not mistaken. Would that be possible?"

"That's right," Molijn answered. "Jung postulates a concept somewhere, which he calls synchronism, meaningful synchronism, to be precise. Is that what you had in mind?"

"What does he mean by that?" I asked indifferently.

"It is mainly something to do with the coincidence of events, two or more events, between which there is no connection for the outsider. For the person to whom they refer, however, they possess a definite meaning, arising from their mysterious affinity which cannot be explained by ordinary logic."

"I remember now," Simone said. "It's like this, Freek. In itself there is nothing special about the fact that there is a man called Joachim Stiller, whether he is mad or not, who amuses himself with the letters and telephone calls we know so well. It need not surprise us either that at the end of the sixteenth century there was a rather unorthodox theologian of the same name. When considered separately, both facts are quite ordinary. But now that we have got to know both Stillers at the same time, well, at least in a manner of speaking, we have the phenomenon of so-called synchronism."

"I understand it. But I don't accept it—at least not without the logical link..." I said stubbornly.

"Imagine for a moment that that Stiller of yours knows the book of his sixteenth-century namesake," my gray-haired friend suggested. "Something like that does not seem at all unacceptable. And what if we go a step further and imagine that he is in fact not quite right in the head and identifies himself in some way with that German wayside preacher? In short, the classical joke about the mental patient who thinks that he is Napoleon..."

"Well, heavens above," Simone muttered. "I say, Freek, couldn't that be..."

"No," I said, filling my pipe, "no. If the man himself had sent me the book, yes...But he didn't send it to me. I picked it out myself here, from a whole pile of rubbish, didn't I?"

Geert Molijn filled the glasses again, unmistakably full of sympathy for this uneasiness, but at the same time trembling with excitement, as if he felt himself for the first time to be in the proximity of a reality, out of reach, but a reality nevertheless, which until this moment he had pursued throughout his life in the most diverse writings.

"Your case definitely fits in with Jung's theory, at least for the greater part..." he suggested.

"It's a pity, but that doesn't get us any further," Simone said wearily. "Nor does it give us an explanation of the business with the carillon, whether it was a hallucination or not."

"No," Geert replied, disillusioned. "Although it is possible that the phenomenon might arise in a much more complicated form. I know that Freek intensely dislikes looking at the affair from a purely occult point of view..."

"Go ahead," I grimaced, "call forth the spooks. It'll have to happen sooner or later. May I have another drink?"

"Help yourself...we won't get around to the spooks for a bit..."

"We must look at the affair calmly," Simone suggested, "especially now that the alcohol is inflaming our imagination somewhat. I don't deny that I get terribly worked up about it. Anyway, we must eliminate all elements that are not directly inexplicable. I would reckon the carillon among the hallucinations. It is probably an accident that a theologian from the sixteenth century bears the same name as our man. The fact that the latter sends us idiotic letters and phones us, preferably at night, may be ascribed to a mental aberration. A certain degree of clairvoyance, which has been observed not infrequently among the mentally disturbed, may explain some of his utterances. Are we agreed so far?"

"Agreed," Geert and I replied at the same time.

"Right. Now that we have reduced the affair to its simplest proportions, one point still remains unsolved..."

"Wiebrand Zijlstra's little man?" I guessed.

"That's true, Freek, I had forgotten about him. But there is, after all, no absolutely concrete impediment preventing the poor wretch knowing something about Joachim Stiller, just like us. Are we agreed over this once again?"

"What is factually possible, need not necessarily be true," Molijn suggested, as if he was afraid that Simone was occupied, with mathematical precision, in robbing the case once and for all of its magical, though frightening, splendor.

"But I didn't mean to interrupt you, my dear, please forgive me."

"In my view the unexplained point is the date stamp on the first letter. Setting aside Schoenmakers' opinion, that stamp could have been faked of course, because it is surely obvious by now that this man Stiller spares no pains or effort."

"You're right," I admitted. "The fellow is so stubborn that it need no longer surprise us..."

"And yet I believe that it is precisely there that we have to look for the heart of the matter. Perhaps I have an exaggerated faith in science, but as far as I'm concerned, Professor Schoenmakers' staff was not mistaken. I don't like it, but I do believe them when they tell me laboratory tests show that it's thirty-eight years old."

I felt miserable. Normally I would have taken much delight in visiting Molijn together with Simone for the first time and, while the summer evening rain trickled down the shop window in the shape of small delta rivers, I would have felt enriched by the knowledge that she too would be at home here from now on, and would thus share even more intimately in my own small and somewhat hermetic world. But it consoled me that, with her fine sensitivity, she understood my disillusionment, and sat down spontaneously on the arm of Molijn's old chair which I occupied as usual, putting her hand on my hair for a moment before replying:

"Reassuring or not, it could be a starting point, even though I don't personally know what to do with it yet...One thing is clear: it has something to do with the problem of time. And well, if you look at it like that...Thick volumes have been written about the problems of space and time. Would it not be wrong to interpret such things one-sidedly as the platonic pastime of some armchair scholar?..."

I saw Geert's face light up, as if he had caught sight of familiar ground again.

"Allow me to go on indulging my imagination on the lines of that suggestion of Simone's..," he said. "In 1919 there was a man who knew exactly what Freek, who wasn't even born then, would write thirty-eight years later in *De Scheldebode* about an event which seemed devoid of all significance. That's one. Secondly, he sent him a letter, which arrived exactly on time, just as if he had written it the evening before, like anyone else sending a letter to the paper. Do you agree with me that time does not seem to exist for our mysterious Stiller, at least not in the way that we are governed by it?"

"That is more or less what I meant," Simone agreed with him. "But once we've got that far, we're stuck irrevocably."

"No, we're not...You yourself have given me the idea. You ought to read Ouspensky thoroughly, *A New Model of the Universe* his book is called, I believe."

"I've heard of the title..."

"Of course, I'm not a trained philosopher...This Ouspensky recognizes only a subjective concept of time for every man as an individual, and rejects the view that time is a continuous line, an eternity before and an eternity after us. In place of this one-dimensional time-line he posits a multi-dimensional concept of time. Proceeding from Hinton's arguments, he even accepts a kind of reincarnation theory."

"Not exactly new," I said despondently.

"But it *is*," Geert continued imperturbably. "According to him, self-awareness does not migrate from one being to another, but after his death every creature begins his own life over and over again; all that has ever happened and ever will happen has already taken place an infinite number of times and will go on taking place ad infinitum. The man who was born in 1890 will be reborn again and again in 1890. We, however, are not aware of this, because we only know three dimensions of a space which has infinite dimensions in time."

Fascinated, I listened. It was of course a hypothesis, only a fanciful and mad hypothesis, but I was gripped by it through its poetic flight of fancy. It was not unlikely, meanwhile, that the gin had something to do with it. A pleasant feeling permeated me, which gradually conquered my fear. I remained nevertheless completely clear in my mind and I knew that there was nothing definite in this victory. Yet the theory evolved by my friend was so surprising that it reduced the Stiller phenomenon (as I called it to myself, suddenly reassuringly objective) to a fabrication for the *Reader's Digest,* something with the title "Rameses II and Nebuchadnezzar Are Still Alive." But while I was secretly amused about Geert Molijn's susceptibility to the most weird philosophies, our host went on imperturbably, blushing with enthusiasm:

"If we don't reject such a concept a priori, the explanation for the things that have happened to you will become conceivable to some extent. In that case Stiller has always been alive..."

"That's not true," I said, "that's not true at all. This rotten Stiller has always been locked up hermetically in his own self-awareness and his own dimension of time—true or not?"

"Come on, Freek, let Geert finish," Simone said; she was obviously worried about the fact that my glass was already empty again.

"Of course," Geert said, "you've got to let me finish, damn it. I haven't finished yet by a long way. Even in the light of Hinton's and Ouspensky's theories our Stiller remains an exception. Ouspensky does not consider it impossible that in the infinite number of time dimensions which form at the same time past, present, and future, some deviations may occur."

"I understand what you mean," I heard Simone say out of the nebulous feeling of pleasure that had taken possession of me. "There are some who escape from their little cage..."

"That's right," Geert replied, "in the sense that the self-awareness splits itself, perhaps an infinite number of times, and at the same time the conventional, I mean the apparently unilateral time, is broken through. In this way the thesis could perhaps be defended that the sixteenth-century Stiller is at the same time the Stiller of 1919, for whom it was not very difficult somehow or other to post a letter which would be delivered in 1957, whereas he is also the Stiller who phoned you last night. No, Freek, don't interrupt me... Perhaps every so-called supernatural phenomenon can be explained at once by the accidental sidelong breakthrough of, well, let me call it the isolation...?"

"It is a beautiful hypothesis," Simone suggested dreamily. "Up till now Stiller's signs of life have never been disquieting. Imagine ... Someone who's broken through his own time shell, dragging his anchor, so to speak, and who is only having an innocent little joke on us."

"Listen, both of you," I said. "Either you are drunk or I am. One of the two."

"Freek is right," Molijn smiled indulgently. "If Simone would be so kind as to give me a hand, we'll have a pot of good black coffee ready in five minutes. Coming, Simone?"

"Marvelous," I grinned. "But walk on tiptoe. What shall I do with my self-awareness if you kick your foot through your private time dimension?"

CHAPTER 15

The Rumor

Psychiatrists and, in their way, confessors are right. Anxieties or fears, once talked over, are reduced to proportions which fall within the limits of what we can withstand without disturbing our inner balance. The next morning, when I went to the paper, everything was more or less back to normal. Wearing a colorful dress with a wide skirt, bare-legged and on stiletto heels, Simone, cheerfully swinging her shopping basket, had walked with me as far as the Groen Square where we had said good-bye, happily anticipating our reunion later.

It was one of those rare summer mornings, as I imagine the summer mornings in the smaller ancient Greek cities to have been, when the sun and the desire for a chat lured the philosophers to the marketplace where the sea breeze temporarily kept their heads cool and susceptible to reason, despite the fact that the hetaerae too were out and about early. I chuckled and lit my first pipe, not without interest in the display windows of a shop for ladies' underwear, and I resolved to let Simone choose a little present for herself pretty soon. Afterwards, she had to laugh when I told her that I had not dared to go in on my own.

Although I was almost exclusively occupied with thinking about Simone and with the recollection of her ecstatically beautiful face—physical in its expression, yet transcending matter—I felt nevertheless deeply fascinated by the morning prospect of the city under its silvery light, misty in some parts, from which one could guess the proximity of the Schelde River. Rarely had I felt physically so completely poised, although I have enough sense of humor to realize that it was mainly due to my male vanity and the pride which I felt at her stammered confession, her face turned away to the window, that she had never known it like this before. I felt as rich as Croesus and as strong as Hercules, completely relaxed, possessed by a boundless gratitude and a stimulating mental clarity,

108

living consciously even in the smallest fiber of my body and at peace with the whole of humanity, as if I had risen, born again, from Simone's arms. For she had kept her arms around me all night, as one does with a child that one wishes to protect from imaginary dangers. But every time I stroked her hip, the smooth plain of her belly or her breasts, carefully so as not to wake her, it appeared that she was only slumbering lightly, as if waiting in her sleep to be woken up like this to make sure once again that it was not a dream, not a snare laid by her wakeful imagination—which at dawn throws us back, poor and bereaved, onto our human loneliness. Up till now I had felt pretty content with life, without expecting miracles. That morning I believed that it was not impossible for a man to be happy, briefly perhaps, but unmistakably happy.

In the Groendal Street I went into the small tobacconist's where I always stock up every other day, without fail. The woman in the shop has long stopped asking me what I want, but this morning she dawdled and even hesitated before finding the packet of tobacco, even though I would have been able to find its place long ago with my eyes closed. After that she got into a hopeless muddle with the change.

"A little out of sorts today, aren't you?" I asked, for why should she too not be drawn into my feeling of harmony with the whole universe?

"Oh, Mr. Groenevelt," she replied anxiously, "one hears such strange things these days. I am only an old woman on my own and in the end one doesn't know what to believe..."

"Believe?" I asked. "Believe? Is tobacco going up?"

"No." She made an effort to smile, "no, it is nothing to do with that... Haven't you heard? All the customers who have been in this morning were full of it..."

"I am as ignorant as a newborn babe."

"You really haven't heard anything, Mr. Groenevelt?"

"Word of honor. But don't try my patience any longer."

"Well..."—for a moment longer she looked at me, helpless and confused, as if she did not dare to pronounce the words—"...people say the world is coming to an end. That is nonsense of course, isn't it, sir?"

"Of course," I laughed, "whatever next? Has there been some story in a paper...?"

"I don't think so...One hears it from another, but no one could say where the rumor came from."

"You sleep quietly tonight," I said. "When I know where this silly story comes from, I'll drop in and tell you..."

My pipe had gone out. I stopped in front of a bookshop while I lit it again. I had just done so when a man who had been standing by the shop window suddenly put his hand on my shoulder. I looked up in surprise. He looked like a perfectly ordinary clerk from some old established firm. He stared at me and I knew immediately that I was dealing with a man whose mind was disturbed. But it is almost physically impossible for me, as a man, to turn my back on a fellow human being.

"Sir," the stranger said, "you must listen to the message," and he continued looking at me in exaltation.

"I don't mind," I replied calmly, "I am prepared to listen to any message, whatever it may be."

He seemed confused by my benevolence, but no more confused than I suddenly felt myself, seized by the inexplicable impression that I had already conducted a stupid conversation like this before in exactly the same place and under absolutely similar circumstances. I could hear beforehand, as it were, what he was going to say, as if we were in a theater where the prompter is racing ahead.

"Forgive me...Are you perhaps an initiate?"

"No," I said, "I don't believe that I am an initiate. I am a perfectly ordinary journalist and, quite frankly, I must ask you to make this conversation as brief as possible, for I have very little time. My name is Frederik Groenevelt. May I know with whom I have the honor...?"

Bewildered, he brought his hand to his forehead, as if he had caught himself committing an unforgivable error. The situation was more comic than painful, despite the almost lugubrious seriousness of the other.

"You must forgive my mistake. But you see, it is my task to remind the people that death can strike at any moment, like a thief in the night..."

"Of course," I said, suppressing my impatience, "it is a beautiful task. Are you by any chance the person who is terrifying credulous souls with idiotic talk about the end of the world?"

Startled by the violence of my words and apparently also indignant, though with irritating reverence, he replied, "You know better than that, Mr. Groenevelt...There is no need for us to tell the people. Since this morning the rumor is spreading by itself, even though the majority of mortals will remain deaf to it, like the people of Sodom and Gomorrah..."

I had had enough all at once and said sarcastically, "Well, that is marvelous, Mr...."

"Angelo," he said.

"Well then, Mr. Angelo, it has been most pleasant to meet you. But now I really must rush..."

He raised his bowler hat with a politeness that had a professional touch—only now did I realize that he was wearing an unfashionable bowler hat—as if he wished to make up for having been tactless and was therefore begging my forgiveness. I turned my back on him and went on my way, not without the feeling that he stood staring after me until I went around the corner. The thought did cross my mind that perhaps I had taken the easy way out, that I ought to have questioned him, for it was possible that he had something to do with the strange events about which I had been continually worrying lately. But then I dismissed such a weakness with determination, irritated at being so easily thrown off balance these days and at letting the memory of Simone, the extremely feminine Simone of last night, be obscured by it. But could I help it if suddenly I remembered Joachim Stiller's book which had been lying on my writing table, untouched since my visit to the library...?

At the paper it appeared that the affair had attracted more attention than I expected. There had been a continuous stream of telephone calls from readers whose imagination had run away with them, kindled by all sorts of rumors, and whose insistence betrayed a panic they could scarcely control.

"It seems a straightforward case to me," Waalwijk held forth. "It is simply the symptom of a disease. The age of epidemics which affected the body is largely a thing of the past in Europe. But we stand at the beginning of a new era, if you ask me—that of the epidemics of the soul. It is a psychological Asian flu. Don't you think, Freek, that there is something in my theory?"

"Absolutely," I said, "but in the course of history, too, such traumatic outbursts have been recorded. Think of the frenzy which overtook the West when the year one thousand approached..."

"That's true," replied Waalwijk. "I hadn't thought of that. The extraordinary thing is that one cannot find a single cause for these idiotic rumors—even if it were only some story about cosmic catastrophes and suchlike... Now we simply don't know where nonsense like this is coming from..."

"Anyway, let's do all we can to reassure the public," I suggested.

"Yes," Waalwijk said pensively, "there's no way around that."

The door of Waalwijk's office was opened and Edgar T'Hoen, the oldest of my colleagues, joined us, sat down grinning, and looked at us mockingly over his glasses.

"We are complete idiots," he laughed. "There is nothing special about the whole story. We forgot that there is going to be a partial eclipse of the sun today. I just remembered a minute ago. It goes without saying that these rumors have got something to do with that."

"Heavens above—the solar eclipse, of course. What do you think, Freek?" Waalwijk asked.

"Yes," I mumbled despondently, as if my happiness of this morning had been merely self-deception; "it seems the most likely explanation. We ought to have thought of it before..."

"It changes the whole case, even as far as the title and the layout is concerned. What do you think of: 'Superstition in the twentieth century. Solar eclipse causes stupid whisper campaign'?"

"If Edgar is in fact right, it would be the best solution," I muttered. "When is that eclipse of the sun?"

"About half past eleven," Edgar said. "I have already put together an article about the phenomenon from a scientific point of view, with the aid of an encyclopedia and details from the news agencies. If the chief agrees, I will embroider the necessary reassuring and, for my part, humorous introduction onto it. But in that case you must go into the city to sniff out the atmosphere and phone through an impression of the prevailing mood about the affair, before we set the type. O.K.?"

"Excellent," Clemens said. "It is the best way to rid ourselves of this insane affair. People seem to be going mad these days..."

In the Pelikaan Street I took the little trolley to the center. I was standing on the front platform and soon came to the conclusion that the sobriety of my fellow citizens is not easily dispelled. No one present appeared to believe in the stubborn rumor though it had spread with the speed of a brush fire, and gibes were continually flying around. After a while it became clear that my fellow passengers—without turning it into an open argument—were making fun of a little old man who was not quite happy about it all and who turned to me, full of resentment.

"I'm just saying, sir," he said stubbornly, "that there's no smoke without fire. It's an old proverb, sir, but it's a good one."

"The eclipse of the sun," I replied reservedly, "has upset some people."

"No," the old man persevered, "no, it has nothing to do with the eclipse of the sun. A while ago I quietly left my house, sir, and imagine, an enormous fellow wearing a bowler hat whom I've never seen before in my life, but who immediately and without ceremony calls me 'brother,' comes up to me and tells me out of the blue that I must prepare myself for a good death. My knees are still shaking, sir. I've got a feeling all the time that a whole lot of these fellows are going about frightening people to death..."

"Nonsense," I said, worming my way out a few stops too early, "it's quite clear you've allowed yourself to be taken in by some joker..."

The doors snapped shut after me and stifled the old man's protestations. I walked quietly from the Royal Palace to the Groen Square. Contrary to my expectations there was not a hint of panic in the air. Apparently the tide of the alarming rumor was already beginning to recede. I did not understand how I could have gotten so nervous about it. Even Clemens's theory about the collective psychological symptom had turned out to be premature. The story of the little old man on the tram had cast a completely different light on my own experience of this morning. In a while, after the solar eclipse, everything would be over, so I did not think it necessary to give my chief editor a special telephone call about it. Gradually it became clear to me that the zealots of some vague religious sect or other must have had the rather bad taste to use the predicted solar eclipse in a naive manner, which had nevertheless caused some panic, in order to spread their ideas with some drastic publicity.

On the tower of Our Lady, the clock which sparkled in the sunlight indicated twenty past eleven. I bought a bunch of white lilies for Simone from one of the colorful flower stalls on the Groen Square, after which I found a seat on the shaded terrace of the "Keizer Karel Café" and ordered a cup of coffee. I had a good view there of the morning crowd and I thought there would be a good chance of Simone passing here on her way home. Suddenly I felt an unutterable need for her company and I was just wondering whether I would try to give her a ring when I recognized alderman Keldermans at the neighboring table.

"I wasn't sure if I had seen right," he said. "May I join you?"

"Please do," I replied. "How are you, Mr. Alderman?"

He looked at me suspiciously for a moment, but there had been no hint of irony in my conventionally polite question. Then he answered, apparently reassured by the expression on my face: "Not so good, Groenevelt, not so good. My nerves, you see..."

"We all have too much to think about," I suggested noncommittally, suddenly realizing that he wanted to confide in me, "and we get excited about a lot of things that aren't worth it."

"Yes," he said vaguely, "yes, you can say that again... There is that story about the end of the world, for example..."

"Come on, Mr. Keldermans," I laughed, "surely you don't believe in that? There is only talk of some little solar eclipse which we'll be able to watch perfectly here from our box seats."

To begin with he had looked pretty smart in his gray summer suit, but now I watched him crumple up again, as it were, like last time, under the weight of some unspeakable fear, reflected mainly in his eyes behind the rather precariously balanced pince-nez.

"I don't know why it is, Freek," he said, "but I feel I can really trust you. Will you allow an old man like me to call you by your Christian name?"

"Yes, please do..."

"Well...I don't believe in the rumor itself, of course. Old Keldermans hasn't sunk that far yet... But when it became clear this morning that the rumor was being spread systematically by people who had stationed themselves in certain spots in the city, the mayor gave orders to the police to keep a watchful eye on the situation."

"A sensible measure..."

"Yes, I agree...The order was issued in strict confidence, but it had hardly been given, Freek, when these fellows literally disappeared from the face of the earth, like rats who smell trouble..."

"Do you really find that so strange, Mr. Keldermans?"

"Perhaps it is because my nerves have gotten completely on top of me...But our police force does not consist of helpless little idiots...It reminded me of that affair of the Klooster Street, you know..."

"I can't really see any connection with that..."

"Listen, Freek. I didn't tell you everything then. I did admit to you that the Klooster Street had in fact been broken up, but I didn't add that on investigation it appeared that no one from our public works department had touched it; at the same time the police officers swore that it could not possibly have been a students' prank or anything like that..."

"That's right," I said, "they were perfectly ordinary workmen— definitely not students, although they were all remarkably handsome fellows..."

"You see...And then I should really tell you the story about the carillon...But well, what's the use...?"

"The carillon? Did you hear it too, that night? I was assured that it was all my imagination..."

I saw great drops of sweat break out on his forehead and bald skull, while he quickly emptied his glass.

"I'll tell you something, Freek," he whispered, looking anxiously around him, "but you must keep it to yourself. You gave me a shock when you said that you also heard it, but at the same time it's a great relief to me. I've already been thinking for some time that I'm going mad or at least that the others are trying to persuade me that I am...I am an honest man, Freek, but if you manage things skillfully as alderman for public works..."

"I understand. You needn't say more than you wish."

"But now I feel safe again. No, it's not like that. I don't feel menaced any more, I mean. At least, how can I express it..."

"Not menaced any more in the same way?" I guessed.

"Something like that," he muttered, "not menaced any more in the same way." He wiped his forehead. "It's going to rain, Freek."

"No," I said, "the solar eclipse, Mr. Alderman."

Scores of passersby, armed with dark glasses or putting their hands over their eyes, stood staring at the purple sky.

The sun still shone, but the light had become weaker, colder, and harder at the same time, almost the color of lead, as if we were at the bottom of a motionless sea where the unwonted refraction estranged us from accustomed things. "The bottom of the sea," I thought stubbornly, "a solar eclipse which makes everything look as if we are at the bottom of the sea," in order to keep at bay the vision, suddenly inexpressibly familiar to me, of a world that had been abandoned to the immobility of time.

CHAPTER 16

The Harlequin in Black

The unsophisticated people who had allowed themselves to be frightened to death by the solar eclipse were not the only ones who heaved a sigh of relief when the phenomenon had passed. Although I had no time to puzzle my brains about it, it seemed as if it had put an end to the period of upheaval in my life which had previously been so quiet; it had been mainly Simone who had steered me safely through this period. It was as if I had gone through an inner cultural crisis, I told her, and I added that history gives very many examples of moments when man is at loggerheads with the cosmos or the inner, mysterious cohesion of things. I dragged Kafka into it and the surrealists, but she, more placid by nature than I, put her finger on my lips and said that she felt happy and that her happiness left no more room for gloomy thoughts.

There were no more disquieting incidents and the period that followed was wonderful for both of us. We did not talk of the future, but it was not because we were frightened of it or doubted the constancy of our feelings.

One morning, when we were sitting down to breakfast, still fresh from the shower, we suddenly looked at each other and said simultaneously, as if under the influence of a telepathic impulse: "What would you think if we...?"

We were thinking of exactly the same thing. That same evening, with the help of Geert Molijn and a driver from the paper, I moved Simone's possessions to my attic which now had a more domestic appearance. I handed in her notice at the same time and promised her that one of these days we would go and see her parents who lived in a villa somewhere between the hills of Brabant and the Campine. She had not asked me, but I knew she longed for this. I wanted to know everything about her from now on, I wanted to know her mother and her father and the house where she had spent her childhood years and her adolescence. She was grateful for it

117

and listened submissively when I rebuked her for not having thought of it herself. She did not need to answer; I knew very well that she had not wanted to force me to do anything before the time was ripe. I had not given up my idea of going to Paris, but August did not seem the most suitable time, so we decided to wait till the first week of September. In the morning or the afternoon—depending on the arrangements of my work at the paper—we took a ride in the car or wandered through the city, which Simone did not know thoroughly enough for my liking. In the evenings I wrote quietly for a couple of hours, while she read my books, washed socks, ironed such a quantity of slips, panties, and similar things as never failed to astonish me, or was busy in the kitchen preparing food for the following day. Sometimes in the morning we would walk to the promenade along the Schelde River and have breakfast there, close to the vigorous bustle of the unloading and loading of the ships bound for the Congo; after that we would start wandering on foot through the old dock area itself, a world almost unknown to her, which filled her with enthusiasm.

During one of our walks near the Royers lock we discovered, hidden behind a lumberyard and huddled against a dike, a little old sailor's inn, situated on a grass-covered road, which still had a rural appearance and seemed to be a relic from the time when it was still all countryside. We drank decent coffee from the family pot which made up for the intrusive anachronisms of the jukebox and the electric billiards. After that we climbed on top of the dike which widens toward the water into a lower, semicircular miniature peninsula bordered on the left by the opening of the lock through which flat-bottomed vessels passed continually, and on the right by a rather shabby pleasure-boat harbor with more wrecks than seaworthy boats, where the primitive palisades, planted in the shiny silt, reminded us of a Japanese print. It was a beautiful day and the rising tide was almost at its height. Fascinated, we sat watching the ships pass by, surrounded by industrious tugs; we spelled their names and home ports on the sterns while Simone secretly stroked my chest under my sport shirt, until she put her arms around me and paid full attention to kissing me on the mouth in full view of the commercial fleet from five continents. There was no indication that my fear still lay constantly at bay, waiting only for a pretext to plunge its treacherous claws into me again. As we were walking home, straight through the area of the old docks, my bewilderment broke lose again and I felt myself tense up inside with a breathtaking shock, as if my whole being—relaxed until now —had suddenly frozen solid like stagnant water. I trembled so violently that Simone, who was walking beside me holding my arm, felt it and looked at me in consternation. I pointed out to her a dark blue poster on the wall of a warehouse which had only one word on it: "Stiller"—innocent, challenging, and obsessive. And at the same time I felt the rigidity melt away and make room for a bottomless emptiness while, as on that morning in the library, my blood hammered with dull thuds against my eardrums. Once more the absurdity of everything I had recently gone through was brought home to me with such force that I wondered in all seriousness whether I was permanently perceiving the outside world out of proportion; perhaps my senses were deceiving me and I was the victim of a persecution complex, forever growing in intensity, about which Simone, perhaps in collusion with Geert Molijn, had wanted to keep me in ignorance to save me from feeling humiliated. However, I felt too dejected to ask questions, not reassured in any case by the fact that, looking around me with a hunted feeling, I noticed numerous similar posters on hoardings and walls. But it could not be a hallucination, for Simone said, "It is nothing... Really, Freek, it is of no significance at all. Some publicity stunt which has nothing to do with us. I am convinced that... But look for yourself— Didn't I tell you?"

The one poster she showed me among the many others stated rather more reassuringly: "Circus Stiller," accompanied by the usual gaudy pictures with which circuses normally announce their presence—beasts of prey, acrobats, elephants standing on their hind legs, clowns, fire-eaters, sword swallowers, short-skirted girls on horseback, Eastern dancers as naked as decency will allow, jugglers, and all kinds of other artists. Taking no notice of the passersby, Simone laid her hands around my face and looked at me imploringly, but without a hint of fear in her eye.

"Can you see now for yourself, that it has no significance? Surely, one cannot imagine anything more innocent and peaceful than a circus? Of course you had a shock, Freek... I got a shock myself, to begin with, at least. Come on, let's have a drink in the first pub we get to..."

The drink did in fact do me good and I felt myself gradually growing calmer. She stroked my forehead as if she wanted to wipe away the wrinkles, but I could not manage more than a painful, forced smile.

"Of course," I mumbled, "a circus ... quite simply a circus. But the name, Simone, why precisely that name?"

"If only I could give you an answer to that ... Believe me, Freek, I have been quite worried too, but this circus is reassuring to me, at least, as far as I still need reassurance. No, I won't leave you alone with your fear. I will never let you down. But my whole being, my body even, has turned against the fear."

"I thought too that it was over, but every time it begins again ..."

"You'll see, it will all come right. Molijn could be right—with his parapsychological and metaphysical theories, I mean. Just regard it as a natural phenomenon for which we will find the explanation in time. And if in fact there is a Joachim Stiller, Freek, well, I am convinced that he is not our enemy. He has nothing to do with Circus Stiller, of course."

Her words did me good. I do not know if I believed her absolutely. But suddenly I was the child of the past again, frightened of the dark and needing to be soothed before going to sleep. There was something consoling in the thought that I could put my fate completely in her hands without feeling shame for my faintheartedness. When she told me, apparently without any ulterior motive, that up till now she had never been able to resist the temptation of a circus, I understood her intention and suggested that we should go together that same evening.

It was a perfectly ordinary circus that had pitched its tents on the Veemarkt in the heart of the Schipperskwartier; the twilight lured dense crowds and the acts of the musicians, clowns, and acrobats on the stage transformed their plebeian wantonness, inspired by the sensationalism of sport and films, with remarkable ease into the eagerness of children, suddenly, as if by magic, unsophisticated and unspoiled again. I was willing to admit that by adding the word "circus" the name Stiller had largely lost its spell and its mysterious significance and that it would be absolutely foolish to try and get information from these good-natured circus folk by groping for connections which could only exist in my overwrought imagination. We found good seats, not too near the arena, from where we could

watch part of the audience at the same time—not the least interesting aspect of the spectacle for me. But I was most interested in
Simone's rapture, the pleasure which she herself drew from her
excited anticipation and the many glances she cast in my direction
as if to express her gratitude for the unexpected outing. It brought
me nearer to the child that she must once have been, the unspoiled
and gentle child that would never die out completely in the
beautiful woman she had become, still surprisingly fresh but at
the same time full of maturity, drawn from the wisdom of the
heart and, who knows, from her body that had been awakened
to conscious life.

Full of elation, she enjoyed the fascinating though mediocre performance, but I felt that it was precisely its conventionality, without a lot of slick gaudiness or showy items, that gave it an endearing intimacy and a refreshing authenticity. She snuggled up to
me as the trainer put his head in the mouth of a lion of pension-
able age, she groaned with fear as the trapeze artists gave the
impression of being about to miss the bars, and clapped her
hands delightedly at the little girl ropedancer from whom we
had bought our tickets at the box office. Gradually I too fell under
the spell of the dynamic display, the blaring music of the small
band, the glitter of the spotlights, the colors, the silver or golden
sequins, and the penetrating smell of the animals. Only when the
director himself gave a display of the classical art of horse training
did I wake up momentarily from my childish intoxication. But it
seemed completely out of the question to me that this corpulent
man of fifty or so with his dyed pointed mustache, top hat and
tight-fitting parade suit could be called Stiller, Joachim Stiller, for
example, or could have anything in common with the faceless man
who had slowly taken possession of my whole being.

Before his demonstration had come completely to an end, or so
it seemed, the clowns entered, accompanied by the traditional
"donkey" with two men inside it. Amidst the loud cheers and the
laughter of the audience they parodied with their infectious pranks
the showpieces of the horseman, who pretended to be most in-
censed, and made them look totally ridiculous. Of the different
clowns I was, for some reason, immediately fascinated by the melancholy Harlequin, dressed completely in black, who acted as the
victim of the others' coarse caprices. He received continuous ap-

plause for the meek resignation with which he accepted his fate, but even so now and then he looked at the audience as if petrified, wondering if he should remain or quickly run away. It soon became clear to me that he was the soul of the trio and that his exuberant partners were merely there to provide the occasions necessary for him to give rein to his tragic melancholia or to get involved in situations which made the spectators roar with laughter, but which at certain moments brought tears to my eyes. Perhaps a generation older than mine had become tired of looking at the man who traditionally receives the blows, I reflected. Yet to me this scapegoat, unearthly and aristocratic in his black satin suit, was an almost tragic symbol of human imperfection and therefore unable to cope with the presumptions of his materialistic fellows who denied him every chance of success by drowning his miniature violin with a tuba, by crushing his white nose under their enormous shoes during a joint exercise in balancing, by refusing to give him a helping hand, so that he would fall into the arena with a humiliating thud, or by treating him in dozens of other ways as a doormat. The audience shrieked with pleasure, by this time instinctively choosing the side of coarseness and the right of the stronger who laid down the law for dreams and poetry, while the pathetic strength of the black clown with his motionless white-powdered mask consisted in tolerating imperturbably all injuries and maltreatment; he was filled with a bottomless gloom but was at the same time supported by the knowledge that those who were planning traps for him did not know any better, and was therefore always inclined to forgive them meekly.

I was aware that the inventions of the trio were nothing much in themselves, but the black Harlequin possessed such dramatic presence, as theater people call it, that he dominated the whole circus tent and gradually began to electrify even the rather unsubtle audience with the mysterious, almost tangible force which emanated from him at a mere glance or a barely pronounced gesture of his sensitive fingers. Next the Little Dancing Girl appeared from an enormous box which the clowns dragged into the arena with a lot of uproar; she appeared fragile and transparent in the brush strokes of a white spotlight. The idyll that followed was mimed by them both with such delicate loveliness that suddenly the whole situation was reversed and the other two who tried in vain to compete for the favor of the beautiful girl fell into all the traps they now laid for their rival. They tried by the craziest breakneck tricks to draw attention to themselves, produced astonishing duets on the most diverse instruments, but did not succeed in tearing the Harlequin and the fluttering dreamlike creature away from a world which remained hermetically sealed against their pedestrian attempts at seduction. Then they decided to take drastic measures. They dragged a miniature cannon out of a second box and aimed it at the unsuspecting Harlequin who had produced his violin again and was playing it in order to express his longing for love that was both serene and passionate. Before the shot was fired the Little Dancing Girl, with a thin cry, noticed the danger and fled from the arena while her melancholy lover himself, irrevocably stricken, disappeared in the dense clouds of loudly banging fireworks, accompanied by blinding flashes of light, a rain of sparks, and a sizzling aura of rainbow-colored stars. When the fireworks stopped as if by magic, the arena was completely empty until the clowns cautiously reappeared. But when a spotlight was directed upward it revealed the black Harlequin on a trapeze right at the top of the ceiling, gently swaying up and down as if his soul was ascending to heaven but was still being held captive by the canvas. Gradually the bar began to swing up and down emphatically and, moving from one trapeze to another, apparently without any physical effort, he seemed to glide through space like a poignantly beautiful, but inconsolably sad bird, until he reached the ground again to the bewilderment of the other panic-stricken clowns. His resurrection and descent were like the triumph of the poetic spirit over material force. And for the first time the Harlequin became beside himself with joy, for the spotlight had carefully scanned the top row of the audience until it reached the place where the Little Dancing Girl was waiting for him among the spectators. He jumped lightly over the enclosure of the arena and danced from row to row like a black, slightly intoxicated night moth, possessed by happiness so delirious that it was almost too great for a mortal being to bear. When he had come quite near his glance met mine. For the first time since the beginning of his act his white face betrayed a hint of emotion and a question flashed through his surprisingly soft, almost feminine eyes. For a fraction of a second we stared at each other. In that short time the feeling surged through me with inexpressible intensity that he was a black angel of death who was about to take my hand in his and enter with me into an infinitely remote and yet nearby world where all fears and problems would fall from me like leaves from a tree in fall.

Instinctively I pressed Simone's arm more closely under mine. But she was unaware of the strange drunkenness which overpowered me and which persisted while the Harlequin continued his half dancing, half floating journey through the audience, until he lifted up his loved one with both arms and disappeared with her —by means of a trapeze which had been thrown toward him precisely at that moment—into the now absolute darkness under the roof of the tent. I was absentminded and not really interested in the rest of the program. I felt instinctively certain that the Harlequin was the same man who had addressed me on the morning of the solar eclipse, and whom I had put off so lightly. Or had I once again lost control of my nerves? . . .

CHAPTER 17

Constellations and Psychopharmacology

People say that nervous breakdowns are a symptom of the times. As far as I am concerned, I get the strong impression that the expression "nervous breakdown" has become fashionable together with a whole store of medical and psychiatric terms. My cleaning woman is convinced that she is suffering from complexes and that there is something wrong with the affections of her youngest child for her. All I mean to say is that up till now I had considered a nervous breakdown to be no more than transitory fatigue or vexation about those small troubles which are totally unimportant but which so often spoil our everday lives.

That evening, however, the breakdown which had probably been lying in wait for a long time manifested itself at last. Up to that day I had always imagined—insofar as I ever thought about it—that something like that only gradually became apparent. I do not know what the doctors think about it. I even remained convinced that my case was not at all serious from a medical point of view—which was later confirmed by Dr. Sergijssels—but of this I am certain anyway: from a still relatively balanced condition I was thrown into a state of unmistakable collapse in the course of no more than a few minutes.

After the circus performance we had walked through the harbor alleys to "De Rode Hoed" at the foot of the Church of Our Lady in order to have a snack there. Simone loves it and I would do anything to please her, for I know that she is most reasonable and would have been just as enthusiastic about stopping at a milk bar or sitting on the terrace of some proletarian tavern, if our budget, which we had been running jointly for some time, had run out. The headwaiter had recommended trout and I ordered a bottle of Riesling to go with it. I still remember that, while I was filling Simone's glass, it started somewhere in between my stomach and my lungs—a tightness which I could distinguish clearly as it unwound itself and quickly spread through my whole body. The center of the rigidity seemed like a knot inside my chest and my throat felt terribly tight; I had only had one glass of wine. I had to force myself not to show how I trembled and how my teeth were chattering; at the same time my heart was throbbing unbearably and a violent panic seized me, rooting itself deep inside me. To this I must add that it was largely an abstract fear without a clearly definable cause; I suppose the thought of Joachim Stiller could not be totally unconnected with it, but I still could not control it in any effective way by reasoning about it. It is true that nothing appeared to menace me, but the world around me was about to disintegrate. It must have been something like what some people rather pretentiously call, I believe, a metaphysical fear.

Simone's presence forced me to keep up appearances as well as I could, even though she was not convinced by my excuse of a stomachache that had suddenly come on. She produced a bottle of tranquilizers from her handbag—so her nerves had also been affected to the extent that she had started using sedatives without my knowledge—but I maintained that it would get better without pills. My refusal had nothing to do with any principles of mine, but rather with the fact that I felt certain—totally without reason—that no one could help me, and with the notion, which I never questioned, that the disturbance had been thrust upon me from outside, like the werewolf in our rural superstition. The wine, however, which goes to one's head surprisingly quickly in circumstances like these, enabled me to observe myself with an amazing clarity of mind. While Simone kept looking at me anxiously and ate only because I insisted that she should pay no attention to my passing indisposition, I made an extreme effort, after the defeatism of a moment ago, to come to terms with the feeling of despair and of being locked up inside myself by looking at it from an intellectual point of view. I tried to persuade myself that I would never be alone again, that only happiness lay ahead of us, that I need not feel frustrated since I was not unsuccessful as a writer, that I was healthy, had a good number of friends and, as far as I could tell, not a single enemy—not even the mysterious Stiller, for he had never uttered any threats.

But at the same time, while prey to a nameless dejection, I

realized that it had all started with Stiller, that he only *seemed* to be totally unconnected with my neurotic condition and that he alone was responsible for the paralyzing feeling of not being able to move forward or backward. Simone firmly held on to my hand as we walked home and it did not escape her that I was shivering as if I was running a high fever. She was surprised when I picked up the phone as soon as I switched on the light.

"You go and have your shower," I said evasively. "There is one element we have so far not added to Stiller's file. I think that a colleague of mine can help us; I mean Jozef Tersago, who concocts the astrological column for the paper every day."

"But Freek," she said hesitantly, but at the same time rebukingly, "surely you don't believe in nonsense like that?"

"Don't worry," I mumbled, "I may be nervous but so far I'm not crazy. Anyway, Tersago does not believe in it himself. He laughs at the nonsense he dishes up for shop assistants every day, but all the same he has studied the subject quite thoroughly, as an amused spectator, let's say, as far as the phenomenological aspect is concerned."

"Would you mind if I stay with you?" she asked hesitantly.

"Of course not," I replied. "If you really want to . . . "

I had picked up the sixteenth-century book and opened it at the passage where Stiller had calculated the time of the end of the universe on an astrological basis. I got through to Tersago right away, for he was on the evening shift that week, and he was most helpful; knowing how he loved to go into rather complicated digressions on the subject, I told him that I only wanted to know what the exact meaning was of the astrological position, which I would slowly read to him. He did not seem to think that there was anything extraordinary about my request.

"It's quite simple," he replied. "A perfectly ordinary description of the present position of the celestial bodies. In short, the astrological situation for the current year. That's all."

It had been my intention not to let myself become upset, but I could hear myself how uncertain my voice sounded when I thanked him.

"Well?" asked Simone, who had not left my side.

"Proof once more that the whole Stiller case is utter nonsense," I said with forced cheerfulness, but I was sure it did not escape her notice how false my good humor was. "Imagine, the end of the world which he prophesied is supposed to be on the Creator's timetable for this year!"

Neither of us believed a word of it, of course—at least, as far as I can tell. But I knew at any rate that Stiller had hooked himself once again, and more firmly than ever before, onto my soul. While I am writing this down, I notice that my story sounds far too reasonable, strictly speaking, if one takes into account the absolute hopelessness in which I felt myself trapped. I was still observing myself with great clarity (was that not a pathological symptom in itself?), but this clarity must have been due to the diminution of my critical insight. If not, I would never have let myself sink to such depths of immoderate and conscious fear of life—or should I call it fear of death? When a sudden attack of vertigo forced me to lie down and my attempt to relax merely had the effect of making me tremble like a jelly, it was Simone who made up her mind and decided for me that I should go and see a doctor the following day. I did not offer any resistance and gratefully accepted her little green sedative tablet. Anyway, I could not care less any more—all I cared about was the anxious expression in her eyes and the certainty, my only and perhaps my last certainty, that her cool hand lay on my forehead.

Although Doctor Sergijssels had a very busy practice and only saw patients by appointment, he insisted during our short telephone conversation that I should come and see him that same morning Normally I prefer to hide behind complete anonymity, if only to stop people feeling obliged to say stupid things about my books which they usually have not even read. This time, however, I did not think it unpleasant that I was not a total stranger to this doctor; he looked about fifty, severe and ascetic and also slightly military, like a tank brigade commander, I thought to myself; but his soft blue eyes amended this first impression to a more precise picture of a rather weary army chaplain who believes that people are unhappy and lonely rather than bad.

"First the routine part, Mr. Groenevelt," he said; he listened to my heart and lungs and wound the black band of the blood-pressure machine around my upper arm. "You simply have no idea how many people think they are having a nervous collapse, when all they have is hypertension. One moment ... That's it ... Yes.

Eighteen ... A bit too much at your age ... But we'll soon fix that. You will feel a lot better when that is taken care of, although there is of course a fair chance that we are dealing here with effect rather than cause ... I will prescribe some harmless tablets and I want you to take them three times daily. You will feel a bit sleepy the first couple of days but that will pass. And let's have a quiet talk now, shall we?"

I admired Sergijssels's businesslike manner and I appreciated the fact that, through his immediate diagnosis of an insignificant organic disorder, he smoothed the way for me to tell of my personal problems, which probably any man of letters who suffers from his nerves considers to be more or less absurd himself. Calmly I told him—and not just "calmly" in a manner of speaking, for since our handshake the fear really had withdrawn into some dark recess—how Joachim Stiller had come into my life, how, with Simone's help, I had resisted his suffocating omnipresence, and how finally my powers of resistance, long since undermined, had suddenly given way like a rotten wooden floor.

"I know, doctor, that I can talk to you without reserve," I concluded, "and you really need not class me among the patients who make your task more difficult through misplaced scruples. I will answer your questions frankly. But it seems obvious to me that you can only help me insofar as my phobia—excuse the technical term which I am perhaps using in the wrong context—originates in myself ..."

"Don't excuse yourself, whatever you do; tell me anything that is on your mind without worrying. I regard you as basically a completely balanced person, Mr. Groenevelt. Above all, you must remember that. In any case, the condition you are in is purely incidental. Your story about Joachim Stiller sounds fantastic, but I do not doubt for a moment the accuracy of what you have told me. I can also understand your reservations. We all consider metaphysics to be naturally a purely academic matter ... But can we be sure we are on the right track?"

"I was afraid you would send me away, doctor. That you would tell me to find out for myself who Stiller is before coming back to you again. I would not have blamed you."

"Although there is no need for you to worry about your condition—always keep that in mind—your case is undeniably one of the

most singular I have ever known. But after all, one could call every
case we psychiatrists treat singular, to say the least. The factors
which cause many an intelligent patient to refrain on purely
intellectual grounds from consulting us for quite a long time—like
your Mr. Stiller—are often precisely those which are decisive in
forming an exact clinical picture—although in your case we are
a long way yet from a clinical picture . . . "

"Can I count on that, doctor? I am thinking especially of my
relationship with the young woman I have told you about."

"Completely. Your nervous breakdown is not even a serious one.
I fear that at worst you have a rather pronounced tendency to
self-torment. Probably a question of education, I imagine—the result
of the irreligious Calvinism of our liberal families . . . Anyway, I
am convinced that in every normal man there is a certain conflict
between the ego and the superego. The faithful are lucky indeed:
through confession they have the opportunity—and this cannot be
praised enough—to be reconciled with themselves. However, a bit
of masochism can't do any harm, I would say. For the present
the main concern is the phenomenon of Stiller . . . "

"That is really why I have the feeling that I am fooling you,
doctor. An outsider *must* think that a story like this is nonsense,"
I said pensively. "I could hardly ask you to accept Geert Molijn's
theories . . . He maintained at one time that Stiller was a part of
myself which had been split off, that I am being confronted with
an ectoplasmic alter ego which is trying in vain to be reunited with
me. He thought it was a marvelous discovery . . . "

"Well," Sergijssels said laughing, but without the slightest trace
of complacency, "we have not got that far yet in psychiatry. And
yet there is a kind of truth in that remark of your friend, Mr.
Groenevelt. I mean, in a certain sense Stiller must be part of
yourself, although I cannot think of an explanation just yet for
his material manifestations through letters and suchlike . . . Meanwhile, you are not a suitable subject for ordinary psychoanalysis.
You know too much about things like that yourself and moreover,
the full treatment lasts a long time and also seems unnecessary to
me. But have you got anything against psychopharmacology?"

"I do not have a very clear conception of what it is exactly . . . "

"Most of my colleagues object to it on ethical grounds but they
are just splitting hairs, although I myself only rarely use it. It boils

down to this, that you lie down quietly and I inject you with pentothal. It stimulates the memory and removes inhibitions."

"It does sound a bit eerie. But we are no longer little boys, after all. Will it make me lose consciousness?"

"Not at all. Some patients say that it gives them a very pleasant feeling. But you must want it yourself, I do not insist."

It turned out to be quite an agreeable sensation. I lay quietly on the sofa, looked expectantly and full of interest at the doctor and felt hardly encumbered by a slight floating feeling which spread perceptibly through my whole body. The only thing that kept me occupied for the present was the question of whether my mind really was so astonishingly clear, or, on the contrary, already muddled, as happens when one is getting drunk but is still enjoying the treacherous illusion of being perfectly lucid.

"That's it then," Sergijssels said. "We'll try the shortest route, especially since we have a good point of departure. Now that the stuff is having its full effect, you must concentrate completely on Joachim Stiller."

"I am doing my best, doctor..."

"Good...What does the name remind you of in the first place?"

"I am thinking of the book Geert Molijn has given me..."

"Right. Just go on talking..."

"It is an old book. It has the nasty smell of dust and mildew. I imagine that it has been rotting away for years somewhere in a cellar. Some of the pages are stuck together. In fact, I am a bit disgusted by it. Geert Molijn's shop also smells of dust, mildew, and damp plaster. His house is rather dilapidated, you see, doctor ...It is one of the few houses that were left standing when a rocket bomb fell near the Lombaardevest—on the Central Post Office, if I am not mistaken. I didn't know Molijn at that time. It is really rather strange...It is strange that since last night I walk around in fear of death, that I feel menaced by things beyond description, by a terror invisible and shapeless—totally preposterous— but that at the time when the rocket bombs were continually exploding over this city I was never really afraid. I adapted myself amazingly well to the circumstances."

Was I awake or was I dreaming out loud, and conscious, out of the inner regions of a quiet sleep?

"Are you quite certain that you have never been afraid?" the doctor asked in an apparently indifferent tone of voice.

Evidently I was not dreaming.

"Once I was afraid. It was a freezing cold winter's day. The bombardment with V-1's and rockets had continued all night, but at daybreak it had become quieter. The city smelt nonetheless as if it were one enormous demolition site where turf fires are lit, and I remember the grinding of broken glass under the soles of my shoes. The bustle on the Teniers Square irritates me; it is teeming with civilians and allied soldiers. I feel that there is something indecent about the fact that life goes on normally in a city that is being bombarded without interruption. I have walked up to here from the paper, because the traffic is totally disorganized. To my annoyance I notice at that very moment that my trolley car is leaving and I start running; but just as I am going to jump onto the rear platform the automatic doors snap shut. For a few seconds I stand panting and irritated on the edge of the sidewalk. At the moment when the trolley car has reached the middle of the square and is about to turn into the direction of the boulevard, I am thrown to the ground by a terrible blow right in my face. At the same time I see a snow-white shooting flame flare up from the trolley, right up into the sky, it seems to me, and the crossroads suddenly has the appearance of a battlefield. I had not heard the explosion of the rocket, since I was inside the vacuum caused by it. But now I hear the terrible animal cries of the numerous victims. There is blood, a lot of blood, running in the gutters, as if they were made for that purpose, and I see torn-off limbs, lying like untidy obstacles on the split road surface. I think I can see a bit further on a body without a head. It astonishes me that one can watch something like this without going mad, and that one can take it for granted that the bodies of the victims, dead or alive, are steaming in the freezing air like the shapeless excrements of enormous flying animals. Then the spectacle is largely hidden from my view as the dust slowly whirls down like a brown mist. To my surprise I have no difficulty in scrambling up. When I feel my face my fingertips are covered with blood, but I know that it is not serious. Only then do I notice the American soldier who, his clothes torn apart, lies dying at my feet. I am completely helpless and do not know what to do; I feel it is a ridiculous gesture, picking up his wallet which is lying beside him. Despite my panic, I decide to wait for help, the wallet clearly visible in my hand to prevent misunderstandings . . . "

"I suspect," the doctor interrupted me, "that you are not telling me things you had forgotten. Or had you forgotten this?"

"No," I said, surprised. "Why, doctor? One doesn't forget something like that. I have only seldom talked about it because it was so dreadful, but I hadn't forgotten. I don't really understand what made me tell you all this . . . "

"Right. Just go on . . . "

"I wait and am forced to watch the horrible spectacle, now that the cloud of dust is slowly settling down. The wailing of the ambulance sirens follows surprisingly quickly. An American truck stops near me, its wheels grinding loudly on the cobblestones . . . But doctor, I . . . "

Helplessly I looked at Sergijssels. I got the impression that he came nearer and bent over me, but I could not be sure.

"Concentrate," he said calmly. "Don't lose the thread of what you are saying."

"I had forgotten one detail . . . A G.I. jumps out of the driver's cabin and I call him over to the dying man who is now rattling softly. Two other men lift him carefully into the truck and do not at first notice the wallet which I want to give to them. Unnerved, I look at the beautiful leather object, terrified that I would be thought a looter. And suddenly I notice the name which is stamped on it in small, golden letters. A moment later I had forgotten that name again, forgotten it for good, I swear. How is it possible that I now know again that . . . "

I felt how the doctor urgently pressed my hand.

"Speak up, Mr. Groenevelt, what was the matter with that name?"

"That name was . . . The dead man was called Joachim Stiller," I said hoarsely, and swallowed with difficulty. "I remember it clearly again. It said: 'Major Joachim Stiller, Longwood, Massachusetts, U.S.A.' . . . "

I sat up in surprise. I had the feeling that my discovery had at once eliminated the effect of the injection. Sergijssels put down his fountain pen, although I did not remember having seen him make any notes.

"Well," he said, "this is a curious result, Mr. Groenevelt."

"Yes," I replied, feeling groggy like someone who has just woken up from a nap in the middle of the day, "do you really believe that...I can recall it all in every detail now, doctor, and I see the letters on the wallet very clearly before me, although the picture of the dying man himself remains vague as it has been all these years. For I am certain that I had not forgotten him. One does not forget a thing like that in a lifetime. But that name, always that same name...Or is it my imagination playing tricks on me?"

"I don't think so. In its simplest form, my diagnosis boils down to this—that you have wanted to push the event away out of your consciousness. Probably the remorse you felt which, by the way, was totally unfounded, because you could not help the man, has fixated itself into a feeling of guilt. But one does not forget what one wants to forget. The name was the only thing which it was possible for you to forget; this would explain the feeling of despondency caused by its reappearance in your life..."

For a while we were silent, like old friends who have no need of words. But I knew better—both of us knew better. Sergijssels was obviously not a man who could not see the wood for the trees. Of his own accord, he went on: "A successful analysis like this would cure an ordinary and even a much more serious neurosis permanently. It is common knowledge, even to an outsider, that in psychiatry the awareness of the cause largely eliminates the effect. But...Yes, how can I express it exactly..."

"You needn't spare me, doctor," I mumbled. "To all appearances nothing has changed, at least, insofar as I, a layman, can form a judgment about it. I would almost say that it has complicated the situation. First there was a Joachim Stiller ouside me; now I know that there is also a Joachim Stiller inside me, who cropped up in my life much earlier than I ever dared imagine. No, it has not made it any simpler. But I am glad nonetheless that I came to see you."

"If I am not mistaken, I am the first one who has discovered at least one piece of the jigsaw puzzle, even if it is impossible for the present to find its correct position."

"That is right, doctor—much more, after all, than I expected when I decided to consult you...You really have helped me. Perhaps it has changed a lot of things. Perhaps you have found the first definitive clue in solving the mystery of Stiller. Who knows, perhaps the Stiller outside me is truly inseparable from the Stiller inside, and this would mean that everything must now proceed on its inevitable course..."

CHAPTER 18

The Traffic Accident

I handed in the prescription from Doctor Sergijssels at the druggist's and then dropped in at the paper. It is not unusual for me to receive mail there, but as soon as the typist told me there was a letter for me I felt intuitively that Stiller had once again shown a sign of life after a silence lasting a considerable time. I studied the envelope hesitantly, but with care. The name of the sender was not on it, but I recognized immediately the impersonal, marvelously perfect handwriting. There was nothing extraordinary about the stamp or the cancellation. The letter had been mailed the evening before, probably at the moment when Simone and I were at the circus. It did not make me feel nervous. The mood of tranquility that had come over me when I was with Doctor Sergijssels apparently had not passed, but I could no longer trust such a relaxed sensation. I put the envelope unopened in my pocket, dealt as quickly as possible with my affairs in the editorial office, and forced myself to stroll home quietly. Letter or no letter, I really believed that the outcome of Sergijssels's amazing examination would be followed by other revelations, and it pleased me that at least I would not have to go back to Simone without any news.

When I opened the door I heard her busy in the kitchen. She had tidied up. There was a bright cloth on the table and she had put a bunch of gaily colored peonies in a brown jar boldly radiant in the slanting rays of the sunlight. The quiet simplicity and also the naturalness of it all filled me with a feeling of blissful peace. I thought to myself that a woman could reverse misfortune and adversity by simple, almost instinctive gestures like these—something a man would never think of. I coughed, like a stranger overcome by shyness in an unfamiliar room, and she appeared smiling, wearing a dress with blue and white stripes which I had not seen before. I got the impression that she had been out during my absence—which was nothing extraordinary, anyway. She put her arms around

136

my neck and looked at me playfully, with a question and, at the same time, a promise in her eyes. I understood that she wanted to make things easier for me after my visit to the psychiatrist.

"It doesn't seem very bad to me," I reassured her. "Sergijssels noticed immediately that my blood pressure was too high. As for the rest..."

My story seemed to be less of a surprise to her than I had expected. She had sat down beside me on the sofa and drew my conclusions for me:

"It certainly does not solve everything. Most of the questions remain unanswered for the time being, but I do absolutely agree that something has been wrested from the mystery. We are no longer completely stuck. Joachim Stiller's life has crossed yours once in the shape of a concrete event—at least, the life, or rather the death, of someone who had the same name. That really cannot have been an accident. It was a good idea of mine to nag you till you went to the doctor." She hesitated and, as if lost in thought, traced with her index finger an arabesque in the faded pattern on the plush sofa.

"I have been to the doctor too, Freek."

I looked at her in surprise.

"To the doctor? I thought you had your nerves completely under control. You are not ill, Simone, are you? Is something the matter? I'm terribly worried...What did the doctor say?" I felt the blood drain away from my face. I was still unable to cope with anything.

"Nothing I did not know already, Freek. I did not want to bother you with it immediately, but there is no sense in keeping it quiet. No, you silly boy, you needn't go pale. I am as fit as a fiddle. As fit as two fiddles even. It is completely natural. I am going to have a child."

She snuggled up against me and nestled her head on my shoulder. As the new awareness gained possession of me, I felt that it was good and that nothing inside me resisted it.

"Let's congratulate ourselves," I said, and we gave each other a long, and not even respectable kiss on the mouth. "And now we are going to get married in a hurry like a naughty couple. I hope it will be a daughter who looks like you, but a boy will do, too... Or imagine...Are there any twins in your family? Only, it's a pity about Paris..."

"Nonsense," Simone said, "not the twins, I mean. But we'll still go to Paris, of course. I am a strapping country girl, you know. Anyway, it'll be months before you can see anything, and when you do, I'll be as proud as a peacock. We've got plenty of time to get married. The only thing that interests me as a practical matter is that the child will bear your name..."

And then, straight through this unmistakable happiness—for I knew for certain now that I was happy because of the child—the deadly fear suddenly bore down upon me again, the fear that the child would never be born, that events were looming over us, so dreadful that man had never thought of them or had at least never seriously considered them. So far I had been able to repress this horrible notion, but this time a frenzied fear broke through the crumbling sand dikes of my last remaining powers of resistance; I broke out into a sweat. I thought I understood with alarming certainty that for weeks I had been throwing dust into my own eyes, but that I had always known it deep inside myself, somewhere in a dark corner of my brain, my glands, or my blood: Stiller meant death, not the personified death of popular imagination, but the abstract idea of the absolute destruction and the end of time for this insignificant grain of dust, somewhere in the border areas of an incomprehensible universe where man had accidentally superseded the silicon compounds and crustaceous lichen. I sat, staring blankly in front of me, mesmerized by this awareness; I was shivering, as if overcome with cold from the Ice Age, and my entire nervous system seemed to be exposed to a high tension which, this time, was going to destroy me. Simone forced me to lie down.

"It is not because of the child," I stammered, "please, believe that it is not because of the child!"

It seemed inexpressibly important to me that she should not for an instant conceive of such a humiliating thought. But she was already bustling around with a damp towel and a flask of gin. The child had been accepted by me, and she knew that I would not go back on that. I felt for the unopened letter in the pocket of my jacket and asked her to read it. As I have already said, fear with me is always accompanied by a great clarity of mind and a sharper awareness of my surroundings. Is it perhaps this fear and sharpened consciousness which enable us, in the hour of our death, to fathom for the first time the meaning of our existence which is slowly flickering toward its end? Breathlessly, I stared at her movingly beautiful face while she calmly tore open the envelope and unfolded the letter. At first she frowned, but then I noticed at once how, very gradually, a smile broke through from beneath her serious expression.

"I believe it is not bad news," she said. "I even believe that this is the beginning of the end to all the misery. You were right, it is a letter from Joachim Stiller, only a very short one. He expresses his regret about the misunderstandings he has caused and says he would like to meet you. He will arrive at the South Station on Friday evening at half past eight. But good heavens, Freek, that is today... He asks that you not wait for him on the platform, but on the square, by the exit..."

She was right. It could only be good news, come what may, for surely there was nothing frightening about a Stiller in human shape who makes an appointment near the South Station like a commercial traveler, in between trains. Slowly the panic ebbed away. I could breathe again, and hope that I would become a normal human being once more.

"Whatever happens, I'm coming with you," Simone decided. "If need be, I'll wait on a café terrace, if you think it has really nothing to do with me, but I'm coming with you. I'm not going to leave you to your fate."

"I wouldn't go without you," I replied gratefully. "I am very happy for you to witness this meeting. Anyway, you are not just a witness, you're directly involved in this whole crazy business. Unless, in your condition..."

"Don't be silly," she laughed, "there is nothing special about my condition. The doctor says that our offspring is doing very well— or, at least, that I'm giving every possible guarantee that he should be doing very well... But there is something in that idea of a witness. Let's phone Geert Molijn and ask him to come with us. Do you think we ought to warn the police?"

"Are you afraid of Joachim Stiller?"

"No," she answered pensively, "I am not afraid of him. I'm even wondering if he does not now fill me with a feeling of trust that is difficult to describe. I am not thinking of Geert because I am afraid. It has more to do with the idea that..."

She hesitated. I took her hands in mine, and urged her to say frankly what it was exactly she had in mind.

"No, Freek, I am really not afraid, believe me. It is just that I wonder if Joachim Stiller, well, if the man who is going to come presently and whom we call Joachim Stiller, is in fact an ordinary human being..."

I did not reply, except perhaps with a vague gesture of my hand, but I brooded over her words all day, even though I preferred not to ask her what she meant exactly. Be that as it may, I had more or less regained my composure. It is true, I was not completely free of fear, but it was a fear "of the second magnitude," as it were. I was especially afraid of the fear that could come back again, a recurrence of the feeling of panic I had just gone through, and the physical defeat which always accompanied it. But I succeeded in keeping control over myself, even if it was difficult, and I clung to the hope that soon everything would be different; meanwhile I was amazed by Simone's self-possession—indeed a typically feminine kind of self-possession. The vague feeling of hope, which I stubbornly repressed in order not to be disillusioned even more when the time came, had already become a certainty in her eyes. Perhaps the riddle could be solved, she seemed to think, so it *would* be solved. I myself, on the other hand, kept brooding over the question as to what new difficulties and vague menaces a potential meeting with the stranger would lead to. Is it possible that for some people a particular fear may last a lifetime? At any rate, I found it reassuring that Geert Molijn was at once willing to accompany us. When the three of us sat in the car which whirred softly over the asphalt with the pleasant purring of an engine which, after a warm day, took delight in the cool evening air, I had some difficulty in dispelling the absurd notion that we were going on a pleasure trip. It was a quiet evening, as honest as a freshly cut loaf, but it was impossible for me to forget the mild evenings which had preceded the outbreak of the war, almost twenty years ago. I felt tense like a tautened bowstring, but controlled my emotion by driving quietly and painfully correctly, as if I was taking a driving test. Simone had noticed, but she remained silent. She was completely calm—I was prepared to take an oath on that— even though, I thought, the time of the inner dialogues between the woman and the child within her body had not yet come. But it seemed to me beyond any doubt that the child had something to do with her composure. Molijn sat sucking his pipe comfortably; for him there was no doubt that Joachim Stiller belonged to a world outside the three dimensions of our ordinary material phenomena, but he seemed to think it was precisely this which was absolutely reassuring—at most a scientific detail which would only confirm what he had always known.

Most recollections of that summer are imprinted on my memory in every detail, but I find it impossible to recall what my further thoughts were that evening in the car as I obstinately devoted my attention to the traffic lights. I suspect that after a while I no longer thought anything. I only know vaguely that I thought at one point —we were driving along by the museum where, on the roof, the bronze horses and triumphal chariots, green with oxidation, caught the last rays of the sun—how it seemed as if I had a radio receiver in my brain, minutely tuned to a transmitter which had, however, been cut out, so that one could only hear a buzzing sound and from time to time a vague crackling.

The South Station was a building of enormous size which seemed totally absurd since all passenger traffic was reduced to the absolute minimum of a few commuter trains, but it lent a suggestively surrealistic air to this stronghold of bygone nineteenth-century progress, the more since it was situated in a rather dead and deserted part of the city which looked moreover as if it had never really come to life. I found it impossible to imagine that Stiller, whoever he might be, would arrive on some local train, mainly used by dock workers on the night shift; it was equally impossible for me to imagine him anywhere, and I had already reconciled myself to the idea that we would soon be returning home, having accomplished nothing, with the prospect of new days ahead filled with shapeless unease.

"Let's turn around and go have some beer in the city," I said gruffly. "This whole business is pure nonsense. We are the victims of some half-crazy impostor who knows better than to come and meet us eye to eye..."

But the others would not hear of it, and I reluctantly parked the car right opposite the station where the café terraces were quite full. Simone and Geert decided between them that it would be best to wait on the traffic island near the trolley stop. This was the easiest spot from where we could watch the exit at a short distance and perhaps ascertain which of the travelers corresponded most to the picture each of us had formed of Stiller, at least, insofar as one can speak of such a picture: I myself had none. The old gentleman who looked exactly like Leopold II had given way long ago to a vague, faceless shadow—something like a painted portrait that had hardly been started.

I did not pay any attention to the other people who were apparently waiting for a trolley, until I found myself suddenly face to face with alderman Keldermans. He could not avoid me, although I got the impression at first that he was trying to. The most confused and contradictory suspicions whirled through my head.

"Well, well, Mr. Alderman," I said ironically, without the others hearing, "what a strange coincidence, don't you think? Getting a breath of fresh air?..."

It was not difficult for him to convince me, although he did not realize what was going through my mind, that he was no old lunatic, no half-crazy conspirator who had set a trap for us.

"God, Freek, how glad I am to see you," he replied, surreptitiously looking around him. "I must ask you to do something for me. Don't leave yet. Stay with me. I'm feeling threatened. I have an appointment at half past eight which I feel I must keep, but I feel threatened nonetheless."

He was perspiring so much that his thin hair clung to his skull in streaky wisps when he took off his hat to wipe his head. But I would have known without these physical symptoms that this man was not lying. He became deathly pale when I asked him flatly, although my legs were trembling as if I had been walking for hours: "Joachim Stiller?"

He nodded.

"My friends and I are here for exactly the same reason." I looked at my watch. It was twenty past eight. "We don't have much time left to discuss it, Mr. Keldermans. Strange letters, were they not? And mysterious telephone calls?"

"Yes," he said. "I thought I was going mad. Hardening of the arteries, the people said with whom I talked about it—behind my back, of course. Do you know who Stiller is?"

"No. But I will think of him as a joker till the bitter end..."

"That is impossible, Freek. He knows things which are beyond the realm of human knowledge. Perhaps we shall never know who or what he is. But I cannot get rid of the thought that I shall not be able to bear the sight of him, that he will ask me to account for ... I don't know what ..."

"Pull yourself together," I ordered him, even though I did not feel very brave myself, "it cannot be long now—that is, if he is going to appear. I will introduce you to my friends. You need not feel embarrassed. They know everything, at least, as far as my side of the story is concerned ..."

I was even more perplexed to see how calmly Simone and Geert Molijn took the whole affair, when I introduced the alderman to them and added that he too belonged to those who were summoned— a badly chosen word which frightened me for a moment, but which did not disturb the other two. I admired the sensitivity with which Simone took pity on the old man, and announced that I was going to inquire where the train, which was expected to arrive at half past eight, was coming from.

"You are mistaken, sir," the man in the ticket office said, "there won't be another train now before ten o'clock. You can rely on that. We don't get that many trains these days that I could be wrong."

The others simply would not consider the possibility of going home. They were prepared to wait until ten o'clock, if necessary.

"It is now exactly half past eight," Geert said, "and you never know. But in any case, we don't seem to be getting anywhere. I wonder if ... But, heavens above, do you see ..."

Breathless, we looked at the exit, about seventy-five yards away. A slim, clean-shaven man in a light gray tweed suit appeared quietly out of the semidarkness. He did not carry a suitcase and held his hat in his hand. I could have sworn that he was of Jewish descent, in spite of his blond hair, and he moved with a perfection so quiet and natural that he suddenly reminded me of an angel. If that stranger really was Stiller, I thought, trembling with emotion, all our fears had been absolutely unnecessary. This man could not be an enemy, he could only be a friend, the bearer of a message so important and at the same time so esoteric that he had no option but to prepare us slowly for it, yes, or even put us to the extreme test, if it had been necessary. Although I could only stare at the stranger, I felt beside me the almost tangible attention of my companions, and also their amazement, like the amazement, once, of the two travelers to Emmaus. But I was the only one whose joyful amazement was also recognition, recognition of the man whom I had watched once, as he lay dying beside me on the sidewalk amidst the dust and blood after the chaos of a bombing raid, and whom I had not been able to help. I experienced joy and amazement—but I felt no bewilderment; I was certain that this lonely traveler could be none other than the stranger for whom I had been waiting these past weeks, perhaps all my life, with a passionate impatience I had never before been aware of, and whose arrival made me feel as if I had been set free at last.

The stranger, in his turn, had noticed us. He smiled, as if he too recognized me from the past, and made a brief gesture, hands spread out and turned up toward us, as if he wished to thank us even from afar for responding to his summons. Quietly he approached. As he crossed the road—the only thing that still separated us from him—I had the feeling that he, a long-lost twin brother, took possession of my impatient soul. He was now only a few yards away from me and my eyes lay already on his large, inexpressibly soft eyes. I gasped with emotion. He said: "I am Joachim Stiller!" and stretched his hands out to me, even before he stepped onto the traffic island.

Never would I press his hands, his brotherly and peace-bestowing hands, in mine. I heard Simone give a scream which rent the heart before I realized clearly what was happening. By a hair's breadth I escaped the army truck which flashed past at a crazy speed and crushed under its wheels the stranger who in hardly a few seconds had given new significance to my whole life. Molijn, Keldermans, and I stood there as if petrified, but Simone groaned frantically, the back of her hand pressed against her mouth to stop herself from screaming out again in horror. Then the thought of the child within her forced itself to the front of my mind, and this proved sufficient to wake me from my brief stupor. A crowd had gathered around immediately and I pressed Simone in my arms, as if to shield her from the curious mob. I pulled myself together, for I was afraid that my helpless inertia might have sprung from cowardice; silently I entrusted Simone to Geert Molijn and with my shoulders and elbows forced my way to the edge of the sidewalk through the crowd that had gathered. The dead man lay across the trolley tracks like a serenely smiling Crucified Christ with his arms spread out and his hands helplessly turned upward; his face, uninjured, was turned toward the still pale summer evening stars. Then someone wearing a cap knelt, bending over him, and said that he was dead. I had known it from the first moment, had felt it right through the horror, as I know now, without any doubt, that it could not have been otherwise. That Joachim Stiller did not belong to our world, but that his appearance was fated to cross our lives like a shooting star, only to die away again immediately, as shooting stars do. Simone had become calmer. She tried to smile through her tears and whispered that I need not worry about her. At the same time the police car and ambulance appeared with deafening sirens from opposite directions, like two bustling giant beetles.

CHAPTER 19

The Third Day

It was after midnight when Keldermans, Molijn, Simone, and I left the police station. She leaned heavily on my arm, but it was above all a gesture of loving understanding; after the first shock she had shown exemplary self-control and had forced herself to be calm with a strength of will which amazed me, as if this was the way in which she could protect the second life, still frail, within her body. Meanwhile, the recording of our official statements had not gone smoothly by any means—at least, to start with. Although he controlled himself, apparently in view of alderman Keldermans's presence, the inspector simply would not accept that we knew next to nothing about Joachim Stiller.

"All right, I can see that the victim had no papers or anything on him by which we could identify him," he said in a bored tone of voice. "But you cannot convince me that the four of you were waiting for him, while the only thing you knew about him was his name—and you say you cannot even be absolutely sure about that."

I had been forced to tell him reluctantly how we had come into contact with the deceased person, and how he had never disclosed anything more than his name in his letters or during his telephone calls. It was only with difficulty that I was able to convince the inspector of our absolute sincerity and good faith, while thinking it wiser to remain silent about all inexplicable aspects of Stiller's behavior. What would a not unintelligent, but sober-minded, policeman have thought of the story about the seventeenth-century book, of the mysterious accomplices of the dead man who pulled up the road surface of the Klooster Street, of the letter about it which had been posted in 1919, or of numerous other details which sounded so unlikely that he would probably have dismissed them as utter nonsense? We were interviewed separately, but the alderman and Simone made statements similar to mine, without us having to agree on details beforehand; Geert Molijn merely said

146

that he had come with us because he had been curious to know who the mysterious stranger might be.

Although it was quite clear that the affair thoroughly irritated the inspector he did not make the case more complicated for us in the end than it already was, considered by itself. Our quiet unanimity, the fact that Keldermans was an alderman, together with my social status and that of Simone—a teacher of mathematics and a journalist not completely unknown even to policemen—seemed to convince him in the end that we were not fooling him or keeping anything from him. I was prepared to talk with him tomorrow or the day after, when I had regained my equilibrium, about the more mysterious aspects of Stiller's appearance in my life, for there were still dozens of questions left unanswered which would not give me any peace for the present. But tonight, in this dreary police station with its cold light, only hard facts were called for, I thought to myself, the hard facts at which our materialistic world stares itself blind without making room for the spirit and the dream. It turned out to have been the right course of action, for even the inspector seemed to feel the need in the end to discuss his views of the case.

"You must forgive me for keeping you so long. You understand that it is my duty to establish the identity of the victim. After all, one has to consider the human side of it. The relatives should be informed right away... but I am afraid that, as it is, the next-of-kin will have to learn of it from the newspapers..."

"Next-of-kin?..." I mumbled, "next-of-kin?...Of course, you are right, Inspector. I really wish I could help you. To be quite frank, I did think in the beginning of going to the police, for the letters and telephone calls I told you about made me very nervous."

"It is not that we did not trust you enough," Simone said; her intuitive knowledge of human nature seemed to give her a certain sympathy for the policeman who, she felt, was bound to fail. "But after all, those letters and telephone calls were not anonymous. He normally mentioned his name explicitly and there was never a hint of threats or blackmail. On the contrary, they were friendly letters, although we could not make heads or tails of them. In retrospect, you are right if you say that we should nonetheless have contacted the police. But what would you or one of your colleagues have thought if we had come up with an improbable story like that?"

"Indeed... You might well have been told that the police have more important things on their minds...Your evidence is of little use but no one can blame you for that. It seems quite obvious to me that we are dealing with a disturbed person who apparently meant to do no harm. After all you have told me—and you will be so kind as to sign your statements in a moment—it goes completely without saying that your curiosity was sufficiently aroused, on the other hand, to make you keep your appointment with this man. I will not detain you any longer. If there are any more questions I will ask you to come down to the police station..."

"There is still one detail I wanted to ask you, Inspector," I said. "What happens in these circumstances with..."

"The mortal remains, you mean?" I nodded. "They were taken to the city morgue." Silently we took our places in the car, still completely under the spell of the horrible accident that had given such an unexpected turn to the strange events of the last weeks. I made an effort to recall the wondrous sensation which had filled me when I saw the stranger's eyes and hands and the way in which he had come to meet me, like a brother who after many years returns home from remote lands—one has forgotten how he looks exactly, but the common blood is stronger than the eyes and one knows unerringly that there is no chance of a mistake. I had seen his blood, his brotherly blood that had slowly flowed from his body, from his still smiling mouth and even from his hands, his blood that had colored the indifferent road surface crimson and slowly seemed to fill the trolley tracks. It did not make me shiver, but a profound sadness came over me which was not altogether free from a feeling of liberation. It had nothing to do with the thought that from now on there would be no cause to be disturbed about Stiller's messages—I wondered if his death had in fact put an end to these —but more with the mysterious, completely inexplicable awareness that he had not died for nothing, that it had thus been preordained since the beginning of time and that he had known it himself—the inexorable necessity of an inevitable sacrifice to make it possible for us and, who knows, for other people too, to go on living. No one made any objections when Geert Molijn asked us to come in for a moment. Even Keldermans did not seem to want to do anything else but stay with us for a while. I knew definitely now that he was a lonely old man whose human integrity had been much less affected by the exercise of his authority than I had imagined up till now. He seemed to have a fatherly affection for Simone and I felt a strange sensation when he said:

"You need not be jealous, Mr. Groenevelt. Miss Marijnissen reminds me of my little daughter. She was only fifteen when she died. That terrible bomb attack on the Teniers Square, you know..."

"Jealousy is not my weakest point, Mr. Alderman," I smiled wearily, "and your affection for Simone makes me happy. She is worth it, you know. It seems as if, after Stiller's death, we have a greater need for human affection than ever before. The memory of that strange man will bind us together for the rest of our lives. There is something consoling in that thought, when you think of it."

"It all started earlier than you perhaps imagine," Simone continued in my place. "When that terrible thing happened to your little daughter, Mr. Keldermans, Freek was quite near. Beside him, an American soldier lay bleeding to death. His name was Joachim Stiller..."

It did not even seem to surprise our new friend—for I knew that the alderman would be our friend from now on, in spite of the generation gap between us—although he shook his head in incomprehending resignation. Geert Molijn had produced a bottle of brandy.

"It seems out of place in the present circumstances," he confessed, "but we all need it badly. I don't think any of us want to go to bed just yet, but we are all completely overwrought. It is healthier than medicine..."

The alcohol brightened us up a little, and I saw Keldermans's gray complexion gradually fade away.

"If only I could understand it," he muttered, "if only I could see any connection. It begins with a street which is simply pulled up by some jokers, and it ends with a dead man on the trolley tracks. Perhaps understanding is too much to ask for. I only wish we knew that it had not all been in vain. Suddenly I have the feeling that I am partly responsible for the death of that unhappy man, even thought I don't understand that either..."

"I'm afraid that we cannot help you," I said. "If I am right, Joachim Stiller's main significance to you was that he sent incomprehensible letters to you too and that he frightened you by his telephone messages. Is that right?"

He nodded. "At first I thought it was an underhanded campaign by my political opponents. I have also thought of the possibility that he was a madman. I wondered if I was perhaps going mad myself. In the end it seemed like a persecution complex. I no longer trusted anyone—even you, Groenevelt, I did not trust right away..."

"Through thick and thin I clung to the idea of a joker," I replied. "But deep down I knew that I was kidding myself. There has to be a limit even to the possibilities of coincidence. I pictured the coincidence geometrically—two intersecting lines: the Joachim Stiller of the seventeenth-century book, the dead Joachim Stiller, and me accidentally standing at the point of intersection... But no Stiller who wrote me a letter even before I was born, delivered on time after nearly forty years, no Stiller whom I saw killed by a German bomb... And I don't even include the pathetic wretch at Wiebrand Zijlstra's who in his death agony whimpered his name, the man who said his name was Angelo, the circus or the black Harlequin with his extraordinary glance, suddenly filled with recognition..."

"I wonder if the police will identify the man," Simone said hesitantly.

"What, for example, if it appeared that those who had known him well attributed exceptional psychic powers to him? Surely that is possible, Geert?"

"It is possible... I have thought of nothing else since the day you confided in me... I have even taken the trouble of writing down all the conceivable theories which indirectly could throw any light on the problem. Look... a notebook full of scribbles..."

I glanced through the notebook the book dealer handed me; it contained mainly references to authors, unknown to me, of parapsychological and metaphysical concepts which did not make me much wiser. But after a while I noticed a sentence in shorthand which I could just about decipher.

"What do you mean by: *Was Stiller not always Stiller?*" I asked.

"Just an idea... At one point I wondered if he had not manifested himself somewhere else, at other times and to other people, probably under another name..."

I shivered, not with fear, but because somewhere deep inside me, infinitely deeper than any human awareness, a vague and elusive inkling quivered through me, of something I could find no words for and which evaporated anyway like ether before I became aware of it.

"It is a possibility I had not thought of... Who knows? But I don't understand the next sentence either: *Fruitless attempts to break through the wall.* Did I decipher that correctly?"

"I must have scribbled down something like that... You must not blame me, Freek, for not bothering you with every idea I had. You were both *so* depressed at one point..."

"I believe you were trying to say something important there," Keldermans said, and I suddenly recognized in him the politician who does not miss a single detail in a debate. "But you will have to help us..."

Geert Molijn pensively rubbed the palm of his hand over his chin. "How shall I describe it exactly... That too was only an idea that came to nothing in the end. Let's see... It was natural that, as an outsider, I regarded the whole business completely differently from you who were directly involved. It was much easier for me to ignore the purely emotional aspect. I understood your fear but I did not share it, not because I was indifferent, but I could see no reason for it. There was nothing to indicate that Stiller wished to do you harm. For me, there was only one clear fact. I did not know of course who and where Stiller was and we do not know that now. But I felt certain that he was making a frantic effort to convey a message to you."

"No one doubts that," I interrupted my old friend, "and he seemed to have the most incredible means of doing this. He could even disrupt Time, if he had to."

"That is right," Molijn agreed. "He had means at his disposal which passed beyond our imagination. But I came to the conclusion nevertheless that somewhere between you and him there was an impenetrable wall. He did not succeed in making himself completely understood..."

Simone had been listening attentively. Her voice sounded controlled: "I think I understand you. You mean that he spoke a different language from ours, in spite of the ordinary words he used, a language which we have never completely deciphered."

"Will the riddle ever be solved?" I muttered dejectedly. "Shall we ever know who Stiller was and what was contained in his message, which was undoubtedly extremely important?..."

"I am thinking more and more that we shall never know," Simone said pensively. "There are too many obscure questions for which we shall never find the solution. I did not want to draw your attention to it, Freek, the evening you phoned Tersago, the astrologer from the paper, because you were in such a bad way already...Do you remember that in Stiller's book the planets Uranus and Neptune were mentioned...the teacher in me pricked up her ears while you were phoning, you see. Uranus was discovered only in 1781 and Neptune in 1846..."

When I think back to the first days following the death of Joachim Stiller I clearly recall every time the feeling of nameless sadness which filled us. Only now did we realize how the stranger had formed an inseparable part of our lives, always present in the background of all our thoughts and feelings. I knew now that the day would have come eventually when he would have vanished again completely into the unknown elements of space and time, enigmatically perhaps, but without leaving this emptiness that would seem overwhelming to me for some time, as if something was permanently lacking in the universe. We had long since ceased to ask for a natural explanation. For the dead body of an accident victim in the modern refrigerator of the morgue, still waiting for identification, seemed to us much less natural than a Joachim Stiller, or whatever his name might be, who had withdrawn from the magnetic field of our powers of comprehension to the silent hinterland on whose coasts human intellect and human imagination must irrevocably run aground.

We would have known a dream which perhaps would once have given our lives a glorious significance, unless a day had come when we had asked ourselves the deadly question if even that dream could have been a dream within a dream. But there was a dead man, a human being with a silent heart and empty veins whose sober description appeared in all the papers, although the press only asked for information and did not go into the matter any further. Evidently the police had only given very little information, probably out of consideration for alderman Keldermans—as if it was some small scandal which had better be swept under the carpet. There was a dead man, I said, whom I regarded involuntarily as a superfluous link and whose presence, even at a distance, made it impossible for Simone and me to relax completely—for it was impossible to call a numb resignation like ours a feeling of rest; it was something like pain wrapped in cotton, empty and inconstant all at once, like the prospect of an irrevocable farewell after which existence would forever lose all its meaning. We did not talk about this and imitated in vain the familiar gestures of before. But even in our most intimate moments—even by day we sought oblivion and consolation in each other—or while we were making plans for the future the thought of the lonely dead man was continually there.

Simone was the first to break the silence, vaulted by words and gestures. I was grateful to her from the bottom of my heart. Once again she proved to be the stronger of us two.

"It does not help to try and forget on purpose," she said, the third evening after the accident, including the evening of the meeting. "I know there is nothing we can do for him now, but we must not keep on with this simulated indifference. It is not right. Neither Keldermans nor the inspector has given a sign of life. How long will he remain lying there with that gentle, helpless smile, while no one cares about him?..."

"You are right," I answered, and put my hands on her shoulders. "Perhaps the ancient human customs in such circumstances have a deeper meaning than we generally imagine. Would flowers be allowed in a case like this, flowers or a last good-bye?"

"I know nothing about these things... We ought to phone Keldermans right away. If he is prepared to come with us, they will not refuse to let us in to say farewell to a dead man..."

"A man...," I said pensively, with an odd feeling, "a man... but anyway, I cannot allow you to come with us this time. You are a woman who is expecting a child. What would the doctor say?" She looked at me calmly, grateful for my thoughtfulness, but at the same time with that determination, totally devoid, however, of recklessness or arrogance, which I loved so much in her.

"Don't think that I regard it as a pleasure, Freek. But I know that I *must* come with you to say good-bye to him. I will be an obedient woman to you for the rest of my life, not out of narrow-minded weakness or self-interest, but because you mean more to me than I can ever tell you. But this time you must let me have my way..."

I phoned Keldermans immediately; he had no hesitation in leaving a council meeting to talk to me from his office in the Town Hall. I had the feeling that my request corresponded with his own wishes, although he might not have found the courage for such an enterprise of his own accord. He promised immediately to do all that was necessary to enable us to give the dead man a last farewell from this world in a dignified manner. We arranged that I would pick him up at his home the next morning to save him using his rather conspicuous official eight-cylinder vehicle.

It was the first time that we slept peacefully since the evening of the accident, although that night a brief but violent thunderstorm broke out. Next morning, before we picked up Keldermans, we bought a beautiful bunch of white lilies without giving details to the salesman of what they were for, so that he would not make a funeral bouquet out of them. It was raining for the first time after many dry days, but when we got out of the car at the Stuivenberg Hospital the sun broke through the clouds. We waited in the gloomy corridor between the street and the courtyard, while Keldermans went to the director's office. I came to appreciate more and more the simplicity of this man who just would not dream of announcing himself with the least display of official dignity. Before we had the time to start wondering about his long absence, a servant wearing a uniform cap came up to us and asked us to follow him to the director's office where the alderman was waiting for us.

His pallor frightened me—I thought that he had suddenly become unwell. The director too looked thoroughly upset.

"Friends," Keldermans said, and his voice seemed to express an infinite sadness, "I am afraid that we have come in vain. No one can understand what has happened. All doors were locked. The police are still busy in the morgue." With an effort he covered his eyes with his hand, as if overcome by giddiness. I believe that I heard his words, even before he pronounced them: "Last night, on the third day after his death, the body of the man known to us as Joachim Stiller inexplicably vanished."

Silently we walked through the dark corridor toward the now bright sunlight which made the wet cobblestones glitter like polished metal. We knew intuitively that it was all over now. We knew also that, thanks to Stiller's blood on the paving stones and on the trolley tracks, the white summer clouds would continue to float safely like great caravels under full sail through a brightening sky over this world at the edge of an incomprehensible universe. Simone let the tears run freely but nonetheless, with her white flowers, and forgetting our presence for a moment, she looked like a very young bride. And when at last she smiled quietly to herself, I felt that the wordless dialogue with the child inside her had finally begun.